THE DEVIL IN T

'It's not easy being a devil. And it's specially difficult if your home is in a tamarind tree in Madras and you find yourself living in an elm tree in London.'

So Brum feels – he's a tamarind tree devil, or brahmarakshasa, and when he first arrives at 32 Crescent Drive, Wimbledon, all he wants to do is go back to India. But Ranjana, the little girl who first notices him, sees his ruby-coloured eyes, green skin and black fangs, and she's sure he should stay right were he is with her family and friends. And when Brum's homesickness overwhelms him and he has to return to India, he soon realizes that the life of a London elm tree devil wasn't so bad after all . . .

Born in India and educated in both India and the US, Indi Rana has worked in educational and trade publishing in the United Kingdom, the United States and India. She now lives in New Delhi and works as a consultant in communication in rural development. She is the author of several books for younger children and a novel for teenagers.

The DEVIL
in the
DUSTBIN

INDI RANA

ILLUSTRATED BY
MANJULA PADMANABHAN

PUFFIN BOOKS

PUFFIN BOOKS

Published by the Penguin Group
Penguin Books Ltd, 27 Wrights Lane, London W8 5TZ, England
Penguin Books USA Inc., 375 Hudson Street, New York, New York 10014, USA
Penguin Books Australia Ltd, Ringwood, Victoria, Australia
Penguin Books Canada Ltd, 10 Alcorn Avenue, Toronto, Ontario, Canada M4V 3B2
Penguin Books (NZ) Ltd, 182–190 Wairau Road, Auckland 10, New Zealand

Penguin Books Ltd, Registered Offices: Harmondsworth, Middlesex, England

First published by Hamish Hamilton Children's Books 1989
Published in Puffin Books 1992
1 3 5 7 9 10 8 6 4 2

Printed in England by Clays Ltd, St Ives plc
Filmset in Baskerville

Contents

I

Oh, Brum-um-um, I yum-um-um . . .

I T's not easy being a devil.

And it's specially difficult if your home is in a tamarind tree in Madras and you find yourself living in an elm tree in London. Now, I know most of you are going to say: "Madras? Where's that?" And that's the kind of thing which makes it so difficult. When you're a tamarind tree-devil from Madras living in an elm tree in London you have to keep explaining yourself. And that can be a pain in your tongue. I mean that . . . right on the tip of your tongue.

You see, when I speak English in London, which, even after all these years I don't very well, the tip of my tongue begins to hurt. People who live in London speak in explosions, banging their tongues hard against the tops of their mouths: *Tta! tta! tta!* In India where Madras is, we speak very much more softly. But if I were to speak in London as I do in Madras, you'd find it difficult to understand me. So I have to speak Tta! tta! tta! as you do in London. And that hurts the tip of my tongue.

So, as I said, it's not easy being a devil.

But I am one, and what's more, I'm a brahma-rakshasa, which makes me an extra special devil. And because it is hard to say, people call me Brum.

Oh, Brum-um-um, I yum-um-um . . .

No, no, no, I'm not a Brummie from Birmingham. No! Let's get that straight right now. I'm a tamarind tree-devil from Madras, India . . . and . . . Oh, my ten-armed gods! now you want to know what a tamarind tree is! Well, waggle my ears, and go look it up in the encyclopaedia. I live in an elm tree in the back garden of 32, Crescent Drive, Wimbledon. And my elm tree is known as Brum's Tree.

You notice how I call it *my* tree? Well, it is now. It was very, very rough going for a while, because at first I didn't want to live in London. I wanted to go home to my tamarind tree. Oh, for the longest time I wanted to go home, just to go home. Back to my tamarind tree in Madras.

And I did go. Back to Madras, I mean, after about

a year in London, when Ajoy and Ranjana went back to Calcutta.

Yet here I am back in London after all, and I have to say that after a long, hard fight, I'm beginning at last, to like it.

Shameful Sneezes in London

RANJANA saw me first, that terrible morning in London. I'd crept out of my eighth dustbin. I'd been hopping from dustbin to dustbin all night ever since I got thrown into one covered with string and wrapping paper and mango pickle, eight houses down the road.

What a relief it was to have a human being see me! Not many *see* us shadow folk, you know. Some look at us, but very few really *see* us. Ask Ching-An the river fairy who lives in the pond on the Common behind the house. Or Zielinski the gnome who lives under the oak tree next door. Or Tumble the soukoyan who lives Shiva-knows-where. Or even Miss

Pennyworth in the castle beyond the pond. They'll all tell you hardly anyone ever sees them. And those that do . . . how we love them. . . . And what wouldn't we do for them!

So, there I was all wet and limp and tired and bleary-eyed, heaving myself wearily out of the *eighth* dustbin I'd tried to find some comfort in, when I heard this girl say in a high, excited voice: "Ajoy! Did you see that?"

I raised my head and saw a girl of about seven, sitting on a mat in the weak patch of sunshine outside some long glass doors. Scattered around her were bits of coloured metal with holes in them, wheels, nuts, screws, screwdrivers and pliers. Later on I learned they were parts of a Meccano set. She'd made a machine out of the bits and pieces and even then, tired as I was, I could see it was a crafty little thing.

The boy, who was older, perhaps eleven, sounded bored. "What?" he said.

"The dustbin, silly," the girl said. "Didn't you see the lid lift up all by itself?"

"Ahhh! Gerrorf!" the boy said, sounding like a lump of unploughed clod. "Must be a cat inside." And he went back to swinging his arms around and throwing a ball as though he were bowling along a cricket pitch.

I'd often seen boys play cricket below one of my tamarind trees in Madras, and for a moment I thought perhaps I'd just dreamt that horrible journey locked in a box, and at any moment I'd wake up back in the sunshine of my home, with the bark of my tamarind tree warming my poor, chill body.

But then I saw the egg-shells sticking to my arms and the greasy wrapping paper hanging over one eye. I felt the pickle-soaked string around my legs, and I knew, never ever would I, a brahmarakshasa, have found myself trying to make a home in a dustbin full of kitchen refuse in Madras.

"It's *not* a cat," the girl said. "You're just an old grump, Ajoy, that's what you are. You don't believe in anything that's fun."

Just then, with a mighty heave, I threw off the dust-bin lid and it fell with a clang on the ground. The effort was so great that I almost fell back into the dustbin in a dead faint.

"Oh, Ajoy," the girl squealed. "Look!"

The boy stopped swinging his arm and said: "Oh, very funny, Ranjana, very funny. Next time, chuck it into the air and we'll report a flying saucer, okay?"

That's the problem – they stop believing in us as they get older, as they stop believing in that fat, bearded gentleman they call Suntar Klauz or something. And by the time they're adults, they have to invent us all over again because life becomes so dull without us. (Gnomes, they think they invented gnomes . . . that gives sour old Zielinski a chuckle!)

I was hanging on to the edge of the dustbin with my hands and my chin. My fingers and the tip of my chin were beginning to turn a dull blue. The girl was looking at me, and I knew she had seen me, because her brown eyes got bigger and her mouth dropped into an enormous O. For a moment, I thought she was going to scream.

Now, I'm not a pretty sight for humans even when I'm looking my best. So, it didn't surprise me that Ranjana seemed ready to scream.

Hurriedly I brought one hand up to my face and put one finger on my lips, and winked so she'd know I was friendly.

"Oh, Ajoy! Look, Ajoy, it's a devil. It's a tiny, little green devil. Oh, my sacred aunts, it's a devil! Oh, crazy Easter bunnies, it's a devil! Ajoy! Oh, gosh-arootees, it's a teeny, tiny, darling little green devil!"

Now, listen to me well, all you who read this. I forgave Ranjana because she was the first human who saw me in a strange country, in a strange climate. But I will *not* forgive anyone else who calls me a 'teeny, tiny, darling little green devil'. No, *that* I will *not*!

I may be skinny and rattly and green, and I suppose by human standards, small. But to call someone who is one thousand, seven hundred and fifty-eight years old 'darling' and 'little' and 'teeny' and 'tiny', simply is not polite. Think, dear readers, think. Think of how you feel when grown-ups put their hands on your head, pat you and say: "And how's my darling little boy today?" and "Have you been a good little girl and done your homework?" How do you feel? Sick, and mad as hell? Well, just think how an older person would feel if you did that to them, just because he was smaller!

I was still holding on to the edge of the bin with only one hand when something terrible happened. I slipped ... and my finger went up my right nostril!

And I sneezed!

Now let me tell you what happens when a tree-devil sneezes: Things grow ... and we have no control over them!

You see, our business is to help the things we live in grow strong and healthy. But when we sneeze, things grow out of control. And nothing is more shameful to a brahmarakshasa than that.

All around, things began to grow. The dustbin grew a metre. The roses next to it grew fifty centimetres. The stones on the crazy-paving rose up against each other at the seams. Ranjana's Meccano machine grew about double and bent into strange shapes because the nuts and bolts didn't grow at all. The grass on the lawn near the dustbin grew half a metre. The fence on the left of the dustbin grew twenty centimetres and the fence further away groaned and creaked. The bricks on the wall of the house just behind the dustbin swelled and the cement binding crumbled. The kitchen window fell out with a crash ... all of it, frame, glass, handles, hinges and all.

Ajoy was standing far enough away so only his trainers grew a little. But Ranjana's long black hair which came down in plaits to her waist, grew down to her ankles, and the ribbons became like scarves trailing behind her.

"Crii-iiky!" Ajoy said, his arm raised above his head, still as a stone carving in a temple. "Holy-moley-bajoleys!"

And this time Ranjana screamed.

I'll give her credit for the way she screamed. She didn't scream with terror – she screamed with delight. She jumped up and hopped on one foot, then the other, and clapped her hands. Her long, long plaits swished like lazy snakes, and she fell over the ribbons.

"Ahhh! This is stupid!" cried Ajoy.

But even an eleven-year-old unbeliever like him had to admit it was strange to see things grow like that ... and keep growing ... so he tiptoed up to the dustbin to look.

The rubbish in the dustbin had grown more than the dustbin, and I was sitting unhappily on it. Ranjana leaned over the edge of the dustbin and grabbed my hand and pulled me out. I came up to about level with her knees ... that is, when I stood up, which wasn't for long. I sat down immediately, in a heap, right in the middle of her Meccano set, shivering and shaking and trembling and wheezing. I held my nose to keep from sneezing again. I knew I ought to say something to stop things from growing ... something I'd learned at school, but I simply couldn't remember what.

Then Ranjana went down on her knees.

And patted my head!

Believe me when I tell you that was the last time she ever did that!

"Oh! Poor little green devil," she said like a little mother. "Poor, miserable, wet, little green devil. Come, let me take you in the house and get you warmed up."

I leapt up, tired as I was, and stared at her as fiercely as I knew how.

Again, I give her credit for being clever and sensible, because she realized at once what was wrong, and said: "Oops! Sorry, sir."

And that calmed me down.

Her brother said: "*Now* what! Are you talking to fairies and goblins again, you stupid idiot?"

Ranjana turned to him and said: "Why, Ajoy! Can't you see him? Standing here as bright as day? He's a devil. I've never seen one like him in any book."

Ajoy snorted and said: "Silly cow!" and stomped off to look for his ball.

Even in my frail condition I was shocked. Cows are never silly. Would our good Lord Krishna have herded cows if they were silly?

So I was quite pleased that because the laces on his trainers were getting so long, Ajoy fell over them, flat on his nose. He sat up looking surprised.

"But Ajoy!" Ranjana said, "how can you pretend there's nothing here? You saw what happened when he sneezed."

"It must have been a little earthquake or something," Ajoy said.

Earthquake! A little earthquake! Now *that* got me truly mad, I can tell you. Me, a brahmarakshasa, a member of the oldest and most respected race of India's shadow people, a little earthquake! Suddenly, after the dreadful events of the last two days – the death of my old tamarind tree, the problems breaking in a new one; falling asleep on the windowsill, waking up in a closed box feeling my stomach had vanished; dumped in a rubbish bin in a strange new place, all cold and damp – after all that, this insult was too, too much.

I sneezed again!

Haré Krishna! Haré Rama! The shame of it! It was bad enough doing it once … but twice in a row? I could hardly think what my friends back home, my gurus, my aunts and uncles and cousins would say if they heard about it.

Well, since I'm telling this story honestly, I have to tell you what happened next. The fence came down, the dustbin blew apart and there was rubbish everywhere. One piece of the Meccano set shot up the side of the house like a ladder, the grass began to look like jungle undergrowth ... Ranjana's eyelashes grew so long they fell on her cheeks, and she couldn't open her eyes. The top teeth in Ajoy's mouth grew so he looked like an astonished rabbit, and he found he was standing in trainers as big as boats. The whole house shook.

Just then a face appeared over the pieces of fencing lying criss-cross over each other on the left. There was rubbish all over them. The face was round with a snub nose and a mop of ginger hair standing on its head.

" 'Ere!" it said. "Wot's goin' on 'ere?" Then looking around, it said: "You lot at it again, eh? Throwin' rubbish everywhere!"

"What d'you mean, 'at it again'?" Ajoy yelled, but because his teeth were so large he seemed to say: "Fuffoo feef, af if afaif?" He went on, getting redder in the face with the effort: "Ef fuffoo feef, foffif fuffif, fou foofif foaf."

But the round face grinned. "Don't know how to live proper like, do you? Just like Pa says, smelly curry and rubbish everywhere. Ma says we'll 'ave to move if this goes on."

Ajoy tried to run towards the face, cross-eyed with anger, his hands fisted up, but he could hardly move in his big boat shoes.

The face snorted. "Ajoy boy! *What* you *goin'* ta catch at school when this gets around!" It laughed nastily and vanished.

Ajoy looked as though he was going to explode.

I could see the trouble I'd caused, but try as I might, I simply couldn't remember the words to stop things growing, much less make things go back to the way they once were.

When I'm very, very troubled, a red light goes on in my head, and I begin to chant certain words to myself. This calms me down and helps me to think. It's called meditation. I closed my eyes and sat cross-legged and began, "Om namayah Shivam," the name of the Lord is Shiva, over and over. And in a few moments I became a little calmer. One doesn't get to the age of one thousand, seven hundred and fifty-eight without learning a little bit of sense, after all.

And as I calmed down I saw from somewhere far away, and over many years, ten student devils standing in our banyan tree school laboratory in Madras, experimenting with sneezing at plants and flowers and grasses and things. And the word to stop things growing popped right up in my head.

"*Thaammmm!*" I cried, in a voice of thunder.

It worked! At last everything stopped growing. Thaaammmm, just like that. Then, before I knew it I'd said the words to make things go back to normal: "*Chinnapo!*"

It was like a dream. The grass suddenly looked as though a hundred cows had nibbled it flat. The Meccano set zipped into place, and the machine straightened up and began to look as crafty as before. Ranjana's eyelashes fluttered back, and her plaits sprang to her waist. Ajoy's shoes whooshed back from boats to trainers so fast he fell over again with the surprise. The fence straightened up and the window jumped back into the wall.

I assure you, Guru Ramachandran, my revered teacher, should you ever read this account of how I came to be living such a strange new life, that although I shamefully sneezed not once, but twice, from being cold and tired, I also acted well in a time of great trouble. I am not a blot on the name of brahmarakshasas. I am *not* one of your student failures.

Ajoy said: "*Whooit!* There really *is* something peculiar going on!"

Ranjana said: "Of course there is. What did I tell you? It's a little green devil."

And Ajoy said slowly, very slowly, and very reluctantly: "Look, if there *is* something show it to me. Because if there isn't something, that Alec is going to spread stories about this in school and I'm going to catch hell."

Then Ranjana said: "If you please, Mr Green Devil, sir, may I describe you to my brother so he can see you perhaps?"

I could, even then, understand English. After all I'm an educated brahmarakshasa, and English is also an Indian language. I nodded wearily ... what else could I do?

So Ranjana described me to her brother.

She didn't use words like 'ugly', 'green', and 'skinny' and 'scrawny' and 'beaky' and 'red-eyed', and all those other things many children who saw me later did.

I'm green, which I know you think isn't the most attractive colour to be, but it suits us creatures who live in trees. I've got horns on my head, which are my pride and joy. And my ears are huge and flappy, and they move around in the most interesting way ... at least *I* think so. My eyes are tiny and the colour of rubies. Amongst us devils this is considered very fortunate. Other devils have eyes the colour of oranges, or peaches or strawberries, but a ruby-eyed devil ... well ... I don't want to sound smug, but ruby eyes are supposed to be very classy.

My nose is enormous, like a large, overgrown beak. I've got, I think, a dashing smile, but unfortunately, humans who see me seem not to think so. It's peculiar, when I smile they usually faint dead away with a piercing shriek. It must be my fangs that do it. They're long and sharp and black. My friends envy me my fangs which are really rather special. They work very well when I have to hang on to a young tree with everything I've got during a Great Battle of Surrender.

I want you to have a good picture of me so when you do see me, or someone like me, you'll recognize us and not get us mixed up with goblins or elves or fairies and all those other well-advertised folk.

I'm long and thin, and very skinny. You can actually see the bones on my rib-cage, even when I'm well settled in a tamarind tree, helping it to grow. I have huge knobbles on my elbows and knees. My fingers and toes are long and thin, and curl almost all the way around, past my wrists and heels.

All in all, from the human point of view, not a lovely sight. You'll have to admit I'm honest, even though this degree of honesty does hurt my vanity. But amongst brahmarakshasas, I'm known as a handsome devil.

When Ranjana saw me that morning I was dressed just in my lungi, which is like a straight wrap-around skirt, of tamarind leaves. And for a chilly January morning in this strange damp country, it simply wasn't enough. Besides which the thin bark slivers which held the tamarind leaves together were coming undone, and the leaves were tearing here and there. I know I smelt terrible ... pickles and eggs and various other bits of refuse ... *ugh* ... If you think green a somewhat unattractive colour, can you imagine green turning blue? My bones rattled on the tin of the dustbin and my tongue, which is usually a delightful shade of orange, was purple with cold and hanging unhappily out of the side of my mouth.

Finally, Ranjana said: "And you must not call him, 'little' or 'sweet' or 'tiny' or anything. Call him 'sir', he likes that."

And Ajoy said flatly: "Oh, what stupid rubbish, Ranjana," and went off to swing his ball around, his arm going like a windmill. "Can you imagine me telling the boys in school that a skinny green devil made a lot of rubbish in the yard, and after Alec saw it, just happened to make it disappear? You must be out of your head!" Then he stopped and rubbed his brow and frowned. "That Alex!" he said, gritting his teeth, "I'm going to get him, really get him one day ..."

We shadow people of India, like little folk everywhere, are made of the finest material. So fine that when we become visible to humans we are just a little coarser than air. Most of the time we are finer, so we're invisible. Sometimes a human sees us for an instant. If he or she holds the idea of us steady in their thoughts, that is, if a human believes in us, we become very visible to them for as long as their thoughts of us are clear.

Ranjana believed in me. Ajoy didn't.

The blessings of Brahma fall on Ranjana.

3

A Place to Sleep

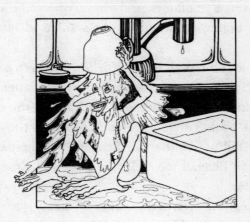

WHAT I have always been grateful for is that Ranjana was a steady and level-headed girl. She wasn't frightened of me or the strange things that had happened. She didn't panic and scream and rush away looking for her parents to help her sort out the mystery. She accepted what had happened, and thought things out for herself and decided on what she was going to do next. Parents can pour cold water on things children see. And I don't mean just when children see devils and fairies and things like us. Children also see other things more truly than grown-ups do, because grown-ups are often more afraid of the world than children are.

She took me into the kitchen which was, oh heaven, warm, and sat me on a bunch of pipes which I later learned was a radiator. And that's where the next problem began, because now she wanted to talk to me.

As I said, I did understand English, and even could speak it a little, though badly. But my best language was, naturally, Tamil, because Madras is in the state of Tamil Nadu, in south India. Ranjana couldn't speak Tamil at all, she was Bengali, but she didn't even speak Bengali too well; she'd been in England all her life.

My English, even today, after so many years in England, isn't much good, and I'm writing this story in Tamil. My publishers, I'm sure, will find an educated Tamil-English translator in this vast city of London, to translate this very important book.

Ahem!

Back to my story.

So, now Ranjana was full of questions: Where did I come from? How did I get here? What did I do? Why was I so hard to see? and so on.

But all I could say was: "Food. Hungry. Sleep. Later, please." And remembering my manners, I was just able to stagger to my feet and join my hands together politely and bow my head and say,

"Namaskar, Chellappa Brahmarakshasa at your service, please."

"Aren't I being selfish," Ranjana said immediately. "You poor th ... I mean, Mr Chellappa, sir, you're tired, hungry and sleepy and I'm just asking you questions ... I must get you clean, and clothed first."

She scrubbed out the kitchen sink, and began to fill it with hot water, but I pointed to a plastic basin and a coffee cup. So she filled the plastic basin, and I got out of my tamarind leaves and, sitting in the sink, sloshed water from the plastic basin over myself with the coffee cup and muttered a few prayers. I soaped myself with some sweet scented soap, thinking next time I'd have to get some good clean earth to wash with. And I began to feel a little better. Purifying oneself with baths and prayers is very important for a brahmarakshasa.

"Have a good soak, Mr Chellappa, sir," Ranjana said. "I'll fill the sink now. It'll wash the tiredness out of your bones."

Well, it was a strange idea, and at first I didn't like the thought of lying down in a sink full of water. "Dirty, dirty," I said.

But when Ranjana pointed out I'd already washed the dirt off and it wouldn't float in the water all around me, I agreed. She was right. After the soak I felt less tired.

She gave me a towel to dry myself, and went

upstairs to fetch some clothes which might fit me. She came down with the clothes off a sailor doll, and sheets and pillows, mattress and quilt off a doll's bed.

I felt a bit foolish in clothes made of cloth, especially with those straight white lines everywhere. But it was better than nothing. The clothes were warmer than the tamarind leaves and I thought I looked quite smart in that sailor's hat, which sat at a tilt between my horns.

The next problem was food. We tamarind tree-devils eat mainly the fruit of the tamarind tree, and drink the juice of tamarind leaves or of bark boiled in water. Sometimes for variety we eat fresh raw vegetables, nasturtium and sesame seeds, and nuts, and herbs like mint, parsley, aniseed and fenugreek. The Bannerjees (which is what Ranjana and Ajoy's surname was), hadn't a kitchen garden. All their herbs and spices were bought from a store and ready-ground and, I thought, stale. The vegetables in the refrigerator seemed wilted and sad, but then, who was I to complain? Ranjana found a bottle of tamarind, pickled in salt, in the pantry cupboard – luckily Bengalis use some tamarind in their cooking as we Tamils do – so I was able to eat a meal of sorts.

Then, the next problem was finding a place for me to sleep. The soothing effects of a bath and food soon wore off and I began feeling horribly dopey again. I didn't know at that time that I was suffering from jetlag, which is what happens to you when you move by air from a country further ahead in time to a country behind in time. You arrive two hours after you've started, but you've actually travelled fourteen or fifteen hours and your body knows the difference. It feels like it's night-time but you're living in the day-time. It takes a while for your body to catch up the lost time.

"Now we have to find you just the right place to sleep," Ranjana said.

Have you ever noticed how, when you enter a room, there always seems to be just the right place for you to sit in? Usually, you go towards that place without thinking about it at all. If you can't find that place you feel terrible. If you think about it too much, you can't find the right place at all.

Well, that's what happened that day.

First of all we tried the drawers in the kitchen. Ranjana laid out the doll's mattress, pillow and quilt. I lay for a while in each drawer, but it was no good. I was too uncomfortable. "Not good," I'd say. "Simply not good for to sleep."

Then we tried the sideboard in the dining-room amongst their special glasses and dishes. Same problem.

We tried the record cabinet. We tried the drawers below the bay window seat.

We went upstairs and tried Ranjana's cupboard

23

and the chest below Ajoy's bed where he kept his old toys.

We went downstairs again. Ajoy came in just then and said: "*Now* what, Ranjana?"

"I'm trying to find the devil a place to sleep," Ranjana said.

Ajoy shouted: "Stupid idiot! Still playing at fairies!" He yanked open the door to the broom closet under the stairs. "Stuff your stupid devil in there!" he said.

It was dim in the cupboard, and dusty, and oh, my good Lord Vishnu! I sneezed again!

I couldn't help myself at all. Oh, how ashamed I was! Guru Ramachandran, my revered teacher, don't think ill of me. I was in a strange country, and very cold and tired ... *that* and only *that* was the reason for my losing control.

Oh, how shall I list the many horrible things my sneeze began! ... Ajoy's nose ... Ranjana's ears ... brooms and brushes ... the pictures on the walls ... Oh, can you just imagine it!

And this time I got mixed up with the words so everything began growing smaller before it had stopped growing bigger ... it was a mess.

Chaos.

Until, finally, from somewhere in my poor tired brain a red light went on again, and I fell to the floor. As my knees folded under me, I began to say the

24

calming words: "Om namayah Shivam, Om namayah Shivam ..." and immediately, as I became calmer, sense returned and I remembered the right order of the words. And got everything straightened out and back to its proper size and shape.

I must record here, that although I was ashamed and horrified, Ranjana enjoyed herself in the most undignified fashion, laughing, screaming and saying things like "Oh, don't stop! Sneeze again, please! Oh, *wowie*! *Whooit*!" and other strange noises. Ajoy just stood there looking quite shaken.

Humans! They really do have everything backwards, I sometimes think.

Anyway. Peace returned.

Then I remembered that I really was an outdoor devil, whatever the weather, and I would never be comfortable indoors.

"The woodshed!" Ranjana said immediately, when I told her.

So, out we went, past the kitchen, the dustbin and crazy-paving. I was so tired Ranjana had to carry me on her back. She opened the door to a wooden shack, and I felt immediately at home. It reminded me so of the houses people live in, in the villages around Madras, except they are made of mud and cowdung. But like them, this wooden shack was small and modest. Do people really need to live in great big brick and stone houses filled with things they don't need, as they do in cities?

There was no wood in the woodshed, of course, because they don't use it for fires in England any more ... they have this terrifying electricity all over the world, even in most villages in India now, though there they still have wood fires.

The sweet smell of earth came up from the floor, and I knew this place would be all right. All sorts of garden things were lying there: spades, rakes and shears, boxes, bits of wood, peat moss in a plastic bag (what will they think of next!) watering cans and so on.

"Yes," I said, my eyes already closing. "This place all right, please."

Ranjana got an empty cardboard box, lined it with the mattress and sheets and all the rest of that ridiculous human rubbish, and I jumped in. Truthfully, I *fell* in.

I can swear my eyes must have closed before my feet touched the box. Certainly before Ranjana left the shed.

But I do remember one clear picture before I slept.

It was a thin, frail, tall tree outside the window of the shed nodding gently in the bleak English sky. And as I drifted off to sleep, I felt a tug inside me, as though the tree were calling, calling to me.

4

The School in the Adyar Banyan

I T was evening when I woke up.

As I stretched and yawned, again I felt that strange tug, and I looked out of the window at the darkening sky. Just as before, I saw that strange tree, now black against the sky, swaying as though it were beckoning me.

The door opened and Ranjana peered in.

"Oh, awake at last," she said. "You know you've slept two whole days and a night. You must be starved."

I said I was, and she produced that same mishmash of pickled tamarind, fruit, raw vegetables and nuts I'd had the first morning. She sat on a wooden box while I ate.

"I've got a problem," she said.

"What problem?" I asked politely. At that moment I couldn't think of a problem bigger than that which I had: I was in a very strange place indeed and somehow I had to get home.

"Ajoy told Mum and Dad I've started talking to fairies and goblins again, and Mum and Dad don't like it. They say I'm too fanciful and imagin ..." she faltered.

"Imaginative," I said.

"Yes, that's right," Ranjana said. "They say I've got to be more real ... real ..."

"Realistic," I said.

"Yes, that's right," Ranjana said. "They say that children who talk to fairies and goblins and things don't do very well in the world and it's time I locked up all my make-believe playmates in a box and threw away the key."

I sighed. This wasn't a new story. Even in India where shadow folk have a revered place in people's minds, as people move from villages to cities, they seem to forget our existence and how necessary we are to the world.

We are the children of Brahma, the Creator of the Universe (which is called Brahman). Brahma's first creations were Vishnu the Preserver (who keeps things going) and Shiva the Destroyer (who gets rid of things which are no longer needed).

Some of us are sent to Earth by Vishnu, only to preserve, and some are sent to Earth by Shiva, only to destroy. This is true of devils and god-lets. *And* humans. But most of us have a little of Vishnu and a little of Shiva quarrelling away in-side of us which often makes life on Earth a great puzzle.

And surely if in India we shadow folk are the chil-dren of the Creator, here too, in this damp and grey country, shadow people must be the same, the keepers of things living and non-living, the very spirit of the world. To believe in us is to believe in the very meaning of life itself.

I said as much to Ranjana.

But she shook her head. "Ajoy says I'm the biggest liar in the world and that it's wrong to tell lies."

I sighed again. All these complicated arguments about what's wrong and what's right and what is lies and what is true, when all that's important is whether what we say or do is wise or stupid.

Stupidity, we shadow people find, is the condition in which most thinking beings live. There isn't much stupidity amongst flowers and trees or mountains and rivers. Very little amongst animals. A little more amongst us shadow people. And a whole lot amongst humans. Stupid people are always doing the right thing at the wrong time, or the wrong thing at the right time. And nothing they do works!

I explained this to Ranjana who seemed to understand a little bit, but like most humans she was puzzled because they are trained to think mainly about what's right, being good and not telling lies.

But a wise person sometimes *has* to do things which are considered wrong and bad and untruthful. It all depends on the problems of the moment.

The important thing is doing whatever is necessary at the time, so it works.

Then I asked Ranjana where I was.

"You're in Wimbledon," Ranjana said, "at 32, Crescent Drive."

"And where's that?"

"In London."

"Oh," I said. "And where's that?"

Ranjana looked puzzled. "Why, in England of course. Don't you know that?"

England! Oh, my good Lord Vishnu! How did I ever get to be here? I'd heard of this far-off land when I was in Madras. But for me to actually be in England . . .

My head began to throb.

Then Ranjana said: "Now you must tell me about yourself. Where are you from and why don't you know where you are?"

Back home when we meet strangers, it's considered polite to tell them all about yourself at once, so they won't have to guess and think you're a strange, mysterious and interesting person. We tell each other all about our families, our work and where we live. We tell about what interests us and what we believe and how much we earn. It's best when we find we have relatives in common. Already I'd been very impolite. Ranjana had been very kind and hospitable and all I'd done was sleep and eat and let her wonder about me.

So, in my broken English and with many wavings of hands and pointings to things to explain myself, I told her:

"My real name is Chellappa. I belong to the ancient race of rakshasas, or devils. I am of the caste brahmarakshasa. We are tree-devils. There are many other kinds of devils: flower-devils and earth-devils, mountain-devils and sea-devils, house-devils and rock-devils.

"I am a pulliyamchedi brahmarakshasa, a *tamarind* tree-devil, so pulliyamchedi is my sub-caste. There are oak tree-devils and banyan tree-devils and eucalyptus tree-devils. Devils for every kind of tree. It's a great honour to be a tree-devil because trees are the most important living things on Earth.

"Some of us brahmarakshasas are sent by Vishnu to help trees grow healthy and well, and others are sent by Shiva when it's time for the tree to die. I am a child of Vishnu."

Ranjana listened to this with her eyes wide open.

"When we're young, we're sent to the Brahmarakshasa Pallikudam. It's a school in the Adyar Banyan, a huge old banyan tree, the oldest in India, in the grounds of the Theosophical Society in Madras.

"When we're being taught the business of becoming tree-devils, our teachers tell us how dangerous a brahmarakshasa's sneeze is. Then, just in case we do ever sneeze, we're taught the word to stop things growing, and a word to make things come back to normal. We test it out in the laboratory. It's quite funny ... can you imagine ten green devils sneezing at plants, stones, brooms and brushes with tiny sneezes and long sneezes and huge sneezes, and things growing jerky or slow or fantastically fast? It gets quite exciting!

It was our favourite class.

"But that was when we were new students. By the time we got to senior school, sneezing was forgotten, as we learned about the speed of rising sap, the shapes of cells and tubes, about chlorophyll and photosynthesis – that most wondrous of all processes which makes plants so unique in the world. Plants are the only living things actually able to make food for all other living things to feed on. We learnt the problems of pesticides and insects, the arts and crafts and sciences of tree-growth – the thousand things we needed to know to become proper tree-devils."

Ranjana finally understood why I was so horrified when I sneezed. But she said: "I don't think it's so shameful when you sneeze. I think it's fun."

Aren't humans strange!

5

Battles of Surrender

Ranjana went on, her eyes glittering. "Wasn't it fun the way Ajoy just wouldn't believe in you even though you almost sneezed the house down!" Then she became serious. "This morning Alec told everyone in school about the rubbish in our yard and he started calling us horrible names. So Ajoy pushed Alec at soccer. Then on the way home Alec got a gang of his friends together and beat up Ajoy, good."

"Oh dear, oh dear, oh dear," I said, quite shocked.

"I wish Ajoy and Alec could be friends, then Ajoy wouldn't feel so bad. I've got lots of English friends, but Ajoy won't make friends with English boys. He just wants to go back to Calcutta where no one will call him names." She sighed. "Mum and Dad also want to go back."

"And why you are not wanting to go back?" I asked.

"Because this is my home," Ranjana said promptly. "I was born here. I'm British. Ajoy and Mum and Dad were born in India. They don't feel British."

"Aha," I said, not quite meaning it. I didn't really understand what she was saying then.

"Can you help Ajoy and Alec to be friends?" Ranjana said again.

I thought about that for a while. Then I said: "We shadow people can be helping those humans who are seeing us. You are seeing me, but you are not having problems. But Ajoy is not seeing me, so what I can do?"

Ranjana thought about this and said: "Maybe Alec can see you. Then you can help Alec."

"That's right," I said, brightening, "but first we must see if Alec is seeing me."

Satisfied, Ranjana then asked me about my work and how a tree-devil gets into a tree to help it to grow.

So I told her about the Great Battles of Surrender.

My first job, after graduating from the Brahmarakshasa Pallikudam was to make my home in a tamarind tree in a village called Chennapatnam, outside Madras. I was given this tree by the Great

Council of Brahmarakshasas.

The tamarind tree was very young, and like many young things the tree was proud and wilful and thought it knew best and didn't need any tree-devil living in it.

I was young too, then, only four hundred years old at the time, and this tree was my first challenge. My first Great Battle of Surrender.

There are many ceremonies to mark a tree-devil's first Great Battle of Surrender. All kinds of tree-devils come together, and there are prayers and feasting and dancing in the open spaces around the tree.

While the feasting was going on I was prepared for Battle. My teeth and horns were filed, and so were my nails ... to be truthful, my claws ... on my fingers and toes. I was dressed in tamarind bark, which I would need to help me grip the tree. A brahmarakshasa priest chanted prayers over me, and all the tree-devils blessed me and wished me success.

Across the field, the tree too prepared for the Great Battle – all the music and noise and devil fires and devils dancers and devil chatter warned it that something was going to happen.

Garlands of marigolds were placed on the lower branches of the tree and around my neck.

A gong sounded. Conches were blown.

There was a cheer, and I leapt upon the tree, and held on to the trunk with everything I had – my teeth, my horns, my claws, even the knobbles on my knees and elbows.

And the tree began to shudder. It began to shake and tremble and sway. It leaned this way and that. It bent over almost to the ground and snapped right up trying to throw me off. Later on in England I saw a movie on T.V. of an American rodeo. Taming the tamarind tree was like riding a bucking bronco. It was exhausting. The devils watching cheered and shouted advice.

This went on for hours, the tree and I locked in a battle of wills. It went on long into the night, a shivering, shaking, swinging, snapping tree with a little devil hanging on, and hanging on, and hanging on under the moonlight into the greying dawn.

The music trailed away, the devils began to snore, and still the tree fought on, and still I hung on using, now, even the bones on my rib-cage to grip the tree.

The sun began to come up, and I was beginning to give in. The battle can go on for days. Sometimes the devil takes a rest for a few hours and tries again later on. Some of my very good friends, like Rajappa and Muthaiyya, stayed up and cheered me on.

The tree gave up before I did.

Little by little it stopped shivering and shaking. Gradually it became still. Its leaves drooped.

Then the pores on its bark opened ... and I was in! I melted into the tree, my cells became the cells of the tree, its sap became part of my blood. We were one. Now I could help the tree to grow.

That was my first tree. My first home, my first job. I got a special mention in the Pallikudam for that, because I'd tamed it in one night.

I had several tamarind trees since my first one, because tamarind trees seldom live over three hundred years. And if they didn't have a tree-devil in them they wouldn't live even that long.

Each time I entered a new tamarind tree, I would have to go through another Great Battle of Surrender. And after the first one, no one came to watch and cheer. It could be a lonely business, doing single combat in the dead of night.

"But how did you come to be here?" Ranjana said. "I mean from Madras to Wimbledon, of all places!"

So I explained it was when I was in the middle of a Great Battle of Surrender with a young tamarind tree in Nungambakkam, a suburb of Madras, that the terrible thing happened which brought me to this strange and cold and grey country called England.

It was a particularly tough young tree. It was not only young, but it was a city tree. And like all city things it thought it knew even better than a village tree. It battled on and on and on.

I had decided I would have to rest for a while before going back to the battle. The tree had stopped shaking and swaying, but it refused to open its pores.

Weak from the fight, I hopped on to the window-sill of the house in the garden of which this tamarind tree stood. And before I knew it I was asleep.

When I woke up ... oh! when I woke up ... Haré Rama! Even now, when I think of it I can feel that awful clutching around my neck, and smell the spilled mango pickle. And even worse, I can feel that empty feeling in my stomach as though everything solid had dropped away from under me.

There was cloth all around me and it was hard to breathe and I couldn't move. Something was sticking into my ribs, and a deep, humming, throbbing noise in the air all around. I was cold, cold, cold.

After many hours during which I slept and woke, slept and woke and struggled to get out of the box I was packed in, the throbbing noise grew louder. There was a pain in my ears; we seemed to be diving down-wards. Then the sound shut off. After a while the box I was in was lifted and thrown, and if I hadn't been packed with cloth all around I would have broken my neck. There was a feeling of being carried along a belt. Straight and then around and around and around. Lifted, thrown, trundled along, lifted and thrown again. Another sound, like that of a motorcar; which I recognized. Miles and miles and miles of this. Lifted again, placed on a springy surface.

The cover of the box was opened, clothes moved around, and I heard a woman's voice say:

"Oh dear! I *knew* this would happen. I just knew it! I told Amma I didn't want to take pickle with me."

And a man's voice said with a great groan: "We've got good pickle in London now, so why did you bring some from Madras?"

"You know how Amma looks at you with those big eyes," the woman said, "as though she's saying: 'Love me, love my pickle!' Oh! Just look at this, just *look* at this mess!"

The box I was in was picked up, and I was thrown with wrapping paper, bits of string, covered with mango pickle, out of the door, and into a heap of refuse in a bin.

As I told this story I shuddered.

Ranjana held her breath as though I was telling her a mystery story. And when I'd finished, she said: "You know what happened? You fell off the windowsill into a suitcase. And whoever's suitcase it was, was coming to London. You were in the baggage hold of an aeroplane, that's why you were so cold."

An aeroplane? Shiva, Shiva, Shiva, who would have thought it!

I'd seen aeroplanes, of course, over Madras, but to actually be in one! It chilled me to think an aeroplane had carried me half way around the world.

Then Ranjana said: "Mrs Narayan down the road at No. 48 just came back from a trip to see her parents in Madras. Her mother always gives her mango pickle. Mrs Narayan always gives Mum some, and Mum loves it. I love it too. South Indian mango pickle's just terrific. Oh, what a pity it spilled." Then she beamed at me and said: "But never mind, I've got you instead. You can be my Indian brownie."

At the idea I shuddered again. I had seen those girls in brown uniform marching around in schools in Madras. What did I have in common with them?

Ranjana laughed when I told her. "No, no, no," she said, "a brownie is a little person, like you. He's English and he lives in people's houses and helps around the house."

But that wasn't me at all!

I stood up straight and tall on the wooden chest in the woodshed and said: "Little Miss Ranjana, have you not ears? Have you not heard me tell you in long way that I am *tree-devil*, a *brahmarakshasa*? My business simply being tamarind trees. Now, if you will please to show me to the nearest by tamarind tree, I will make for myself a new home while I decide how I am going back to Madras."

But Ranjana said: "Mr Chellappa, sir, there are no tamarind trees in England."

And at that moment it became clear to me that I was in deep, deep trouble, for a tree-devil must find a tree within one month after the old one dies, otherwise the tree-devil will wither away.

The thought was so shocking that for a moment I

sat there dumbstruck. Then, because I had to think about it, I said I was sleepy, and asked to be excused. Ranjana nodded and left.

I lay in my box and thought.

No tamarind trees!

I was a tamarind tree-devil, I could not live in another tree.

Could I get back to India?

How?

Fly?

By aeroplane?

Yes, I thought with relief, by aeroplane as I had come. That would be easy. All I had to do was get into the right aeroplane.

And, thinking that as aeroplanes get around quite fast, I had a little time during which to explore, I fell asleep again.

6

An Elm Tree Home

THE next few days were very strange. I slept a lot, ate pickled tamarind, and saw very little of Ranjana. She was at school most of the time, and when she and Ajoy were home, their parents were there too. Sometimes Ranjana came out to see me and we talked about Ajoy's problem with Alec. But I had other things on my mind for a while.

I spent a lot of time prowling around the gardens in the neighbourhood, and behind the houses. To do this I had to take off the sailor suit because as it was made of human material, it would have been visible to human eyes. I shuddered to think how humans would react if they saw an empty sailor suit squeezing through the fences and under rocks and between the flowers!

The first day I wore the suit not thinking what might happen, and a big grey cat jumped on me. It took all my wits to get away without being scratched. It's an advantage to be so thin and agile. My body can curve and bend in ways you would not believe outside of a circus.

I made a lungi from the leaves of the tree at the bottom of the garden, and began exploring.

I didn't know exactly what I was looking for as I scuttled around the gardens, but I knew I needed to know more about the place in which I found myself. I needed to know the flowers and grasses, the bushes and the trees. I needed to know what birds lived there, and whether I would recognize their songs. I needed to know how friendly the frogs were, whether there were crickets that chirped in the night, and what patterns the snails had on their shells. I needed to know the way the wild flowers and mushrooms grew, and what the rocks whispered to each other as the sun went down. I needed to hear which way the water ran, and how the trees sighed in the evening breeze. And what was it the clouds said as they lay in their grey blankets over the land?

Most of all I needed to know whether there were other shadow people like me. Was there a fairy of the rocks? A snake nymph in the pond in the middle of the park? Were there little people living in the trees? Would we talk a language together we understood? Who lived in the old oak tree next door? Was that a devil of the air I saw just then riding on the breeze?

There was much I recognized and much that was new. There were many things that were the same as they were in Madras, and some things that were not. And I can't begin to list them all. But what struck me most was how tightly the houses stood together all around a central Common from which, strangely, all the houses faced away. The gardens were cut off from the park by high fences without gates!

It would have been just the other way around in Madras, all the houses facing the park in a friendly way. What strange people these were, I thought. And how small everything was and how very tidy and clean, how pretty the sloping, red-tiled roofs and bay windows. How weak the sun was here, and how the clouds wept all day in a thin drizzles.

I liked most of what I saw and didn't like some. Guru Venkataraman used to say, back in the Adyar Banyan, that the truly wise man liked everything Brahma created. But I wasn't truly wise. After all, I was only one thousand, seven hundred and fifty-eight years old. Young, for a brahmarakshasa.

I felt the trees call to me, and one day I asked

Ranjana their names. The tree at the bottom of the garden was an elm; a tall, frail, soft thing with gentle leaves. And there were beeches and chestnuts and limes. But nowhere was there a gul-mohur, the flame of the Indian forests, no jacaranda dusting blue in the sky, no simul floating wisps of cotton, no eucalyptus growing straight and tall and strong. No palm trees. And no tamarinds.

The spaces in my body began to long for the touch of a tamarind tree. I told Ranjana one day that soon I would have to go back to India.

"Why don't you move into the elm instead?" Ranjana said in her practical way, "and spend a little time here before you go back? Besides I'll have to think of how to get you into an aeroplane."

But something in me got sick at the thought of becoming a tree-devil for any other tree. I was of the sub-caste pulliyamchedi. My body was made for a tamarind tree. It was as though Ranjana was asking me to take off my skin and put on a new one. It would be breaking my caste rules.

Yet every day I felt the tug of the elm tree. Was there an elm tree-devil I couldn't see living in it? I felt around the tree, it seemed cool and delicate to the touch. I whispered words to make the devil come out. But there was nothing there, so I wandered away.

There seemed to be no shadow people at all in this

crowded neighbourhood. And I began to feel lost and lonely.

One day I went over to No. 48, where I'd first been thrown into the dustbin. I wandered around at the back of the house looking at the nasturtiums growing across a rock garden, a vegetable patch behind a fence, and then went up to the front.

My heart soared! Little people!

There on the front lawn were ten of them, dressed in tall red hats, blue jackets, brown trousers and white boots. They all had big white beards and jolly wrinkled faces. They seemed to be marching around a large mushroom-shaped lamp.

I ran up to them. But oh! the disappointment! They were all made of stone!

When I told Ranjana about it, she shook her head sadly.

"They're stone gnomes," she said. "People put them in their gardens because they miss seeing real little people. There aren't any little people in this sort of neighbourhood any more. They all went away when people began building houses like this so close to each other, and made so many machines. I read in my books they like it where there are fewer people and more trees and natural things. Perhaps there are some still on Wimbledon Common, but I've never actually seen them, though sometimes to annoy Ajoy I pretend I do."

I told her that back at home things were as crowded, but shadow folk lived everywhere. Perhaps we didn't have so many machines, but machines made no difference to little people in India. We believe that even in machines dwells the Lord Brahma. And we keep up with the times. In India there are devils and godlets who look after factories and nuts and bolts and power generators and nuclear reactors.

Two weeks later I began to feel ill. At night in the woodshed I dreamed of the young tamarind tree outside Mrs Narayan mother's house in Nungambakkam in Madras, and how hard it had fought, and how its bark felt to my touch. And I woke just aching to get back home.

Ranjana saw how droopy and unhappy I looked, and she came to fetch me into the house.

"Mum and Dad are out playing cards," Ranjana said. Then she looked at my lungi of elm tree leaves and said: "Aren't you cold any more?"

And I jumped. It was true. In three weeks my body had become used to the cold damp air of London!

"It's getting warmer," I said. And that was true too.

And then I told her that somehow I had to get back to Madras within the next ten days, or I would die.

"Well," Ranjana said seriously, "I could try to put you on an aeroplane at Heathrow, but I couldn't get to Heathrow alone, not even to the Earl's Court terminal. In any case even if I could get to Earl's Court and found out what flight you should get on, you could get lost in the airport. You could spend days just trying to find the right gate, or you would get trampled on. And besides, is there a direct flight from London to Madras?"

"Perhaps somebody will come to see you soon and you could take me to the airport when you go to receive them."

"But that might not happen," Ranjana said.

Then I began to get worried. Very worried.

One day, in desperation I tried getting from Crescent Drive to the subway station by myself, thinking I could surely find my own way to the airport. But I was getting weaker every day. I almost got run over by a huge red double-decker bus, and had to turn back.

The next morning I knew I had just enough strength to try one last Battle of Surrender, and no strength for anything else.

That night I looked at the elm tree nodding and swaying in the chill night breeze, and I went up to it and put my hand on its trunk. I held my hand there for a long time trying to feel the pulse of the tree, the flow of the rising sap. I tried to understand the mood of the tree, and the way its thoughts ran. All night I sat with my back against the tree and turned my ears to listen to its root beat. And by morning I had made up my mind. The next two days I ate only elm tree leaves and drank only elm tree leaf juice.

It was a Sunday morning when I decided to go to Battle. Ranjana's parents were out again, celebrating the birth of a child in the Bengali community. Ajoy was on the Common behind the house playing cricket with some of the neighbourhood boys. Only Ranjana was there to cheer me in my Great Battle. She helped me file my horns, teeth, and claws. I stripped some bark off the elm tree and made up a lungi. I squeezed some of the leaves and smeared the juice over me.

I mumbled a few prayers. Ranjana brought out a conch shell from her mother's prayer room. She blew it hard. I leapt on to the trunk of the tree feeling like a traitor to my tamarind tree training and way of life. I clutched the tree, ready to hang on with all my strength.

And by the good Lord Vishnu, what a surprise!

The tree fought me for only three minutes, and gave up.

It opened its pores and I was in!

It was the strangest feeling in the world. My body cells were tamarind tree cells, and this was an elm tree. They had nothing in common. I seemed to freeze a little. My temperature fell. Something seemed to shift inside me, and then there was a feeling of great quiet.

I wondered, suddenly, who had really surrendered

in this battle. Was it the tree? Or really, was it me?

The elm was a much more peaceful and graceful tree than the tamarind, and once I was in it I could begin to talk to it.

"I'm not a young tree," it said in soft silver tones, "and I'm not strong. I've watched you wandering around and although I haven't known what your business was, I've felt drawn to you. I'm glad you decided to make me your home. We'll both be good for each other."

I stayed a long time inside the tree, getting the feel of its cells, the minerals and the salts, the texture of the chlorophyll, and the rate of osmosis (you can look *that* up in the encyclopaedia). And as I sped between the molecules, I felt my body become part of the tree, and I began to feel clean in a way I hadn't felt since my last tamarind tree had died. Soap or even earth and water are nothing to good healthy tree fluids.

After a few hours I came out of the tree. I suppose to humans who see us it must be a strange sight, because we seem to melt out of the tree. A bit of us appearing first like a little bump and the rest sort of forming behind it as though out of the very fibres and bark of the tree. This happens when a devil actually becomes a part of the tree. When we use a tree just for schools or Homes for Respected Ones, or for meetings of the Great Council, we use the holes and spaces in trees, like owls and squirrels do.

Ranjana was waiting worriedly for me to reappear. She smiled with relief when I materialized.

"Was it all right?" she asked anxiously.

"It was wonderful," I said. "I feel like a new devil."

And of course, I was.

Guru Ramachandran, if you read this book, know that there are indeed stranger things under the sun, as you used to tell me, than your student ever dreamed. It is possible for the devil born in one caste to do the work of another. Guru Venkatraman will surely say I have broken the laws of caste. But under the circumstances, what else could I do? Yes, it was stupid to fall asleep on an open window ledge. But only from stupidity comes wisdom. I was wise to try an elm tree, was I not? Or I should have died holding on to my caste.

7

Zielinski and Tumble

Soon after I made my home in the elm tree, things began to happen. When I look back, it seems as though before I had decided to accept my new home, there was a curtain in front of my eyes through which I saw things only hazily.

Early one morning when I was up in one of the top-most branches of the elm tree, looking at a black patch that had appeared on the bark, I saw a stone gnome standing at the foot of the old oak next door amongst the roots. But then, the stone gnome moved! There was a flash of blue and red, and the gnome disappeared into the roots of the oak.

Like lightning I was out of the elm and over the fence. I peered into the place the gnome had disappeared, but could see nothing at all. Not even an opening. I stood there scratching my head and wondering if I'd just imagined the gnome.

"Stop looking like a klotz," a cross, snappy voice said.

I jumped.

"Here, here," the voice said irritably. "Your eyes are open now. So use them."

"Where?" I said stupidly.

"In your head, of course. Where you think your eyes are!"

"Oh," I said, even more stupidly.

Then I saw there was a little window where two roots joined. It was like a peep-hole in a door, and two bright blue eyes were peering out of it. The door opened and the gnome came out. It was a cunning little door, so well made that if you didn't know it was there you would never have seen it. The outside fit perfectly, gnarled and twisted just like the roots.

"Ach, boze! What a time to be seeing things. So early in the morning. My bedtime!" the gnome mumbled. "Now I must be nice, I think."

He was about as tall as I, and much, much rounder. And very, very alive. His beard shook with vexation.

I had a dizzy feeling of relief. One of the little

54

people! Somebody like me! I wasn't alone!

"So, say something," the gnome said, "don't stand there like a klotz."

"Ahhh ..." I said, recovering myself. "I am ... I am ..." and joining both hands politely, I bowed my head and said: "Namaskar, good sir. I am Chellappa Pulliyamchedi Brahmarakshasa. At your service, sir."

The gnome put both hands on his hips and looked at me like thunderclouds. Like Lord Indra, the God of thunder, lightning and rain, on the warpath.

"Don't give me that gtupot!" he said. "What is your name? I am Zielinski."

"My name is Chellappa," I said. "I am Pulliya ..." I stopped. I was no longer a tamarind tree-devil. "I am devil of that elm tree over there, please," I finished.

The gnome grunted. "What was you saying back there? Brum? Brum something or other?"

"Brahmarakshasa," I said, "that is tree-devil."

"Brum, eh? Brum. Well, Brum, we was all wondering when you would settle, so we could let you see us."

I was astonished.

"But ... why you wait until I am settled?" I cried, thinking how lonely I'd felt and how I would have welcomed little people like me in those first few days. Ranjana was all right, but she was human and humans cannot ever understand what we shadow people feel: second class citizens in a world controlled by humans. "Why did you not showing yourselves before and helping me to settle?"

The gnome cleared his throat and said gruffly: "Yes, yes, yes, we could have done that. But it is difficult to settle into new place. We wanted you to make decision by your own. We did not want you blame us later."

"Oh!" I said, scratching my head again. This was a strange way to think. Back at home we help people all the time. We all feel we are responsible for each other, because being the children of Brahma, we are responsible for the whole of Brahma's creation.

"We helped Ching-An settle," the gnome said, "and she has not forgive us for that. She moan and complain all the time. Oh yes, she say that if we had not help her, she would have go back to Yangtze River in China, first chance."

A little person from China! That was exciting news. In Madras we'd heard of other countries, of course, but we lived in such a small world of our own, with so many rules and regulations, doing things the way they should be done, that we hadn't time to think much about other places, or wonder about other kinds of people, although some of us had been around India over the years.

"We had a African Yo, one time, but he went back to Africa," Zielinski said. "Or perhaps he did. When

I see him last time he was wanting to go to docks and get on ship. Ach! I am glad we did not try to make him to stay."

"I see," I said slowly. And dimly I began to understand that when you are with people you have been with for many thousands of years, we can be closer and more familiar. But when we are with strangers, the rules are quite different. It takes a long time to understand people very different to us, so people move carefully, giving each other a lot of space to find out who they are in a new place on their own. In a way it's a test of determination and character.

A ball of light suddenly appeared from behind the oak tree, and darted between the roots, glowing bright and dim as it moved. Merry gurgles and chuckles rolled out from it. The ball of light stopped just behind Zielinski and began to become dense. Slowly it began to take shape, and little by little, it turned into . . . another gnome, just like Zielinski!

My mouth really dropped open, and I stared like a fool. I had never seen anything like this in my life. I had seen some rakshasas change into humans, or animals, but never a ball of light become the exact image of a person standing near me.

"There you are," Zielinski said, "being a klotz again." He turned around and saw himself standing behind him.

"Tumble!" he roared. "You stop that now!"

The gnome called Tumble shrieked with laughter, and changed, right there, into a toad.

"Rididip," he croaked in Zielinski's voice. "Rididip."

"Stop playing fool, Tumble," Zielinski said, "and become something we can have decent talk with."

The toad changed into ... oh, my ten-armed gods ... into me! I looked at myself standing in front of me, and felt quite faint. He was a perfect copy, from my claws to my teeth, to my horns.

"I'm Brum-um-um, I yum-um-um," the other me said in my voice. He put his hands together and bowed his head, just as I do. Without thinking, I put my hands together and bowed politely saying: "I'm Chellappa Pulliyamche ..."

And the other me fell on the ground and held his sides and kicked his legs and laughed until tears flowed from his eyes.

I stood stupidly looking at him. That was my day to be a klotz!

Zielinski bent over his huge stomach and hauled the other me to his feet, muttering something like "*Mie badz osiolem!*" in a strange language.

And at that moment the tree-devil changed into what I later learned was an English brownie. He was small and skinny and knobbly, with a sweet face which had on it a huge grin. He had a pointed nose and ears, and everything about him was pointed, the ends of his shirt, his chin, his fingers, and the toes of his shoes.

"That is better," Zielinski said, "you are someone we talk to now. Introduce yourself, Tumble, and properly. No more your tricks."

The brownie put his hands in the pockets of his tights, stuck his chin out at me and said in a very un-English way, dipping and raising his voice: "Hey man. I name Tumble. I is soukoyan. I come from Trinidad. In the Caribbean, fah fah away across the sea." And he slapped his thigh and laughed. "Ching-An, doh like me, but Miss Pennyworth think I awright. Hey! Brum, man, we goin' to be fren'!" And he flung an arm round my shoulder and pumped my hand with his free hand.

I liked him at once.

"Well, well, well," the gnome Zielinski said. "Well, now that is done. Tumble, you take over. I go to bed. Take Brum to meet the others, and no tricks. Wait till he know you better." And he vanished into the roots of the oak tree.

"He so fat, and he have such a bad temper," Tumble said, "but the man good."

And that's how I met two more of my own kind in London. They weren't the kind of folk I would have met in Madras, but they were all the more interesting to me for that.

8

Ching-An and Miss Pennyworth

"Now, come, lemme introduce you to the others," Tumble said, taking my arm, "and when you meet Miss Pennyworth an' Ching-An you know all we living here in Wimbledon."

"All?" I said, dismayed. "You mean to say there are only four little people in the whole place?"

"For mile an' mile an' mile," Tumble said cheerfully. "There ah some on Wimbledon Common an' down in Surrey in the country, but the nearer you get to London the less likely you see little folk livin' there."

"But why only here?" I said. "Why only in this

place? It is surely too much coincidence?"

"I doh know," Tumble said. "Maybe it have to do with Miss Pennyworth in that castle over there in the park."

I was surprised. "What castle?" I said. "I have seen no castle."

"Open your eyes, man. Look! There – just behind the pond," Tumble said. "You see the pond?"

"I have seen the pond," I said. "But I have never seen anything in it or around it."

"So look now," Tumble said, and leapt on to the fence which separated the back garden from the park.

I looked. And by the good Lord Vishnu! I saw!

Rising behind the pond, which was now a moat, was a magnificent castle! It had a drawbridge over the moat, high walls, spires and towers, turrets and domes, hundreds of cupolas and thousands of long narrow windows. It was made of some shiny shimmering transparent material, which threw off beams of light, and reflected the grass and trees and the red roofs of all the houses.

I gasped and stared and gasped again.

"Cobweb," Tumble said proudly. "It made of cobweb an' dream. An' it bin there three thousan' year."

"But . . ." I stammered, "why have I not seen this before?"

"Because Miss Pennyworth doh wan' you to, is

why," Tumble said. "Also the difference between looking and seein', is why." He chuckled. "When I first come to this place, I too get the big shock, man."

"Who is this Miss Pennyworth?" I said, dazed.

"She is the direc' decendant of King Oberon, King of all the little folk in this country. She is the last fairy here. All the rest gone away to the country."

We began towards the castle of Cobwebs and Dreams.

"Why is it made of Cobwebs and Dreams?" I asked.

"Because dreams are so importan'," Tumble said, "an' because they so hard to see an' understan'. Is like lookin' through cobwebs, all ol' an' musty." He grinned and looked at me sideways. "Cobwebs are also so fine an' so strong they hold all the dreams together."

There was long silence, then I said: "Oh." I was quite confused.

We reached the pond-which-was-a-moat, surrounding the castle.

Tumble knelt on the grass and shouted into the water: "Ching-An! Come here an' meet the new Mister Brum."

There was no answer.

"Ching-An, you come out of the water right away!" Tumble yelled.

Still no answer.

"She right here in the pond," Tumble said. "She

sulkin', I bet. You wait, lemme get her."

And he leapt into the pond. As he leapt he turned from an English brownie to a fish.

I waited, thinking of the *nagins* back home, who are part human and part snake, of the beautiful water nymphs called *apsaras* who also live in rivers.

A little while later there was a rippling in the water, and Tumble-as-fish came to the surface holding a strand of long straight black hair in his mouth.

He turned into a brownie again, and dragging the hair behind him, walked up to the grass.

"She sulkin', like I said," he said. "The more she sulk, the longer her hair grow."

He pulled and pulled her hair, until there was almost a mountain of it on the grass next to us.

Finally a pale face floated up to the surface of the water. Her eyes were closed, and her lips turned down in a pout. Then her body rose, and she lay long and flat under the water, her hands crossed over her waist, her legs stretched out.

"Come on, lady!" Tumble said, losing his temper. "Jus' come out right away!" The girl opened her eyes and sighed in a bored way. Then she rolled her eyes up as if to say, "Oh really!" turned over, stood up and floated out of the water.

She was wearing a long dress with flowers and birds all over it, tied at the waist with a sash. There wasn't a drop of water on her. She had dark eyes, a short, straight nose, and high, pale cheeks, slim, pretty hands and feet.

"*Nin hau*?" she said in a bored, polite, tinkling voice like little wavelets on the water. Her eyebrows rose and she looked down her nose.

"She say, 'How you keepin',", Tumble said.

I joined my hands together and bowed my head.

"*Yindu ah*?" she said.

"She say, 'Are you Indian?' " Tumble said. "She could speak English but she woan."

"Yes," I said.

"When I go home to China," she said in English, in a royal, superior way, "I shall visit India." Then, as though she had said all she wanted to say for a long, long time, she slipped back under the water. Slowly, her hair slipped back after her, like a snake.

Tumble shrugged. "I doh know what to do with her. We try everythin'."

"How did she get here?" I asked.

"I doh know. She doh speak much. But she keep the pon' clean, and she have a real nice pretty house of weed down there. The frog and insect like she a lot."

He took my arm and began to walk towards the drawbridge.

"How *you* get here, please?" I said.

"I wanted to see the world, man. I get tired of Trinidad," Tumble said, "so I get on a ship in Port of Spain." He giggled and turned a somersault in the air. "Man! I had a great time. I sat on the prow of the ship and everybody thought I was St Elmo's fire!"

"What is that?" I asked.

"Is ball of electric light which sit on the highest point of the ship when the ship in a storm. Some people think is a ghost, and some people think is good luck. I always have a good time. I could change to anything, go anywhere. But I spen' all my time as a' elf or a brownie or a goblin, because Miss Pennyworth miss all them folk here."

"This Miss Pennyworth, she has always been living here?" I asked.

"She sure has, man. She is two thousan' year old."

"And Zielinski? How did he get here?"

"There was some trouble in he country, Polan', an' he come to stay with family. But then, they all move away."

I sighed. "Do you think all those little people are ever coming back?" I said, feeling very lonely.

"Miss Pennyworth tryin' to bring them back. She workin' all the time to make little people come back. She say little people are the spirit of the world. We the creatures of the Great Creator. She say is important little people do their job or else human beings will suffer too much and will make the whole world an' its plants, an' trees, an' water, an' mountains an' everything suffer too.

"She say it bad thing English people make their cities, so English little people go away to the country, man. So Miss Pennyworth happy when little people come. She say it good thing to have little folk wherever they come from. And since there ah so many humans here from the Caribbean, an' India an' China, is good to have little people from there too."

I thought I would like this Miss Pennyworth. I imagined she was a little old lady with about a thousand wrinkles and wise, kind eyes, like some of the old devil-women back home.

As we talked we had walked up the drawbridge, and the castle rose up all around us, with turrets and windows and stairs leading off everywhere. It was silent and empty. Tumble led the way through a passage-way lined with armour, tapestries and paintings into the audience hall. Far at the other end, a great carved gold jewelled throne stood on a dias, empty.

"Yoo-hoo, Miss Pennyworth!" Tumble shouted. The words echoed all around and disappeared into the high ceiling. I could see the rooms behind the walls, and rooms behind those rooms, carpets and furniture and paintings and windows one over the other. It was like standing in a transparent dream. It made me dizzy.

"Com-ming," a fluting voice called back. And through the door behind the throne, a whiff of mauve and pink floated in.

Haré Rama! Haré Krishna! She was the most beautiful little thing I'd ever seen in my life. She had yellow, almost white hair, and green eyes. She was wearing a mauve dress that looked like bits of rags, and the wings behind her were pink and mauve. Like me she was bare-foot, and her feet hardly touched the floor as she came towards us.

"So! At last!" she cried, stretching her hands out and taking mine. "Chellappa Pulliyamchedi Brahmarakshasa, welcome."

Will wonders never cease? She got it perfectly the first time.

"Has Tumble told you all about us? Yes? Good. Now let's sit comfortably and talk."

She led us through the door into a small room behind the Great Hall, and sat us down on big, soft sofas in front of a fire.

"Now, tell me all about you," she said.

So I told her about Madras, the school in the Adyar Banyan, the tamarind trees and the Great Battles of Surrender. I told her about falling into a suitcase, flying through the air, finding myself in a dustbin, and about Ranjana and Ajoy. *And* about Alec. And about how I'd come to be an elm tree-devil.

She listened quietly and asked questions every now and then.

When I told her about flying in an aeroplane, her

67

eyes widened. "Why, what a wonderful thing!" she said. "I've seen them of course – great gnats droning in the sky. I've never liked them myself, noisy things, quite monstrous, but if they brought you here, perhaps they can bring others."

I said: "I am here, Miss Pennyworth, but it has not been easy. I came simply by mistake, and I do not know if I am wanting to stay here for rest of my life. It is very hard to move away from your own people, you see."

"Hmm," she said, her chin in her hand. "That's true I suppose, and I would do nothing to move people anywhere against their will. But humans have always moved around everywhere for one reason or other. And so have shadow folk. Now humans move faster and further because of these aeroplanes."

I was silent.

"People have always longed for a new world," she said slowly, her eyes far away, "new ways of thinking, new ways of behaving. Perhaps, when many different kinds of people learn to live together, we'll have this new world.

"People may have to move from place to place to discover how alike we all are underneath. Then, maybe they will start to think of 'us, all together' and not 'us against them'."

I listened to her, thinking how easy it was for us to live together in and around Madras, where everyone knew who they were and what they had to do. Why was it such a problem here?

"Remember," Miss Pennyworth went on, as though she had heard my thoughts, "the whole world belongs to everyone, not just to the few people who have lived in the same small place all their lives. But today we have to think big because our world is becoming smaller and problems in one place affect everyone, everywhere."

My good Lord Vishnu, I thought, listening to Miss Pennyworth, you sent me to Earth to be a brahmarakshasa, to do my little part, taking care of tamarind trees, and that's all. But here is this pink and mauve fairy asking me to think about everyone and everything. I'm not sure I'm big enough to do it.

Then Tumble said quietly, without his usual chuckle: "We all will have to be bigger in our heart than we used to be."

Slowly, I looked up from the floor. "Those are wise words," I said.

"Wisdom," Tumble grinned, "never came easy, man."

And suddenly I felt very, very happy. These were my kind of folk, we talked the same language.

"But, stupidity," I said, and Miss Pennyworth and Tumble and I finished together, "is the easiest thing of all."

And we all laughed together.

Then Miss Pennyworth said: "When you are sure you want to stay here, Chellappa Pulliyamchedi Bramarakshasa, we will ask you to work with us. Until then, find your way in peace."

I went back to the elm tree that morning feeling happier than I had been for many, many weeks.

9

The Troubles of Ajoy and Alec

HAVING met four of my own kind, the very next thing that happened was that I ran slap up against the problems of Ajoy and Alec.

It happened like this:

Ranjana knocked three times on the lowest part of my elm tree one morning, just near the roots. This was the signal we'd agreed on, if she wanted to talk to me.

"I'm off to school," she said, as I materialized. "You want to come?"

When I looked doubtful, she said: "Oh come *on*, Brum. You've been stuck in this neighbourhood long enough. Come and see what the wide, wide world looks like."

She was right. It was time for me to move away from the security of my tree, the garden, house and Common.

"You can ride in my satchel," she said. "I've left space for you."

So while she fretted and Ajoy fumed about missing the school bus, I tidied up a few things inside my tree, and hopped into her satchel. I sat on top of her English Reader and her lunch box, and peered out under the flap.

Ranjana and Ajoy hurried around the corner to the main road and joined a group of children waiting at a bus stop.

Oh! Oh! Amongst them was Alec, the boy next door.

When he saw Ajoy and Ranjana, he made a face, and moved deliberately away from them. He leaned towards a friend he was with, and whispered something in his ear. Then both of them looked at Ajoy and Ranjana and giggled. Alec then made a loud, long rude sound with his mouth.

Ajoy looked ready to burst with anger.

Ranjana held his arm and said: "Don't pay any attention to them, Ajoy!"

Ajoy rumbled something in his throat.

Luckily, just then the bus came along and there

was a scramble to get on. Alec and his friend were right up in front and Ajoy and Ranjana at the back, so for the moment everything was calm.

It was a most interesting ride, I can tell you! After so long keeping to my neighbourhood, I felt as light as air, looking at streets and streets of semi-detached houses with their bay windows, at the High Street full of shops and goods in them we couldn't dream of having in Madras. We zig-zagged down the streets, stopping to pick up children. The din in the bus became terrific. My nose got quite flattened against someone's back.

The school was a series of concrete, flat-roofed buildings set in a concrete yard, fenced off with high wire fences. There was hardly a tree in the entire school yard! I was amazed. What were they up to, these British? How could children be taught anything of value when there were no trees around?

Ranjana's classroom was quite pleasant, with big windows, clean wooden floors, lots of desks and posters and models on tables all around the walls of the room. I thought of the scrubby earth floors children sat cross-legged on in most schools around Madras, with hardly a book between them, only a bored old teacher and scratched old blackboard to help them learn anything. How lucky these children were ... except when they looked out of the windows and saw no trees. In Madras, there were trees at least.

Ranjana's class had reading and maths, the first two periods. My word that was interesting! The teacher asked them to read, and then asked them questions and they had discussions. In the maths class, the children didn't even have to recite their tables! There was constant movement and talk, not like in Madras, where children were not expected to do more than learn what was taught to them, keep quiet and never question the teacher, who, because she was a teacher, was always right!

Then there was a break.

Ranjana got her bottle of milk, and dragged the satchel, with me in it, into the yard, to drink it with a friend.

"How do you like it so far?" she asked me under her breath.

"Very, very interesting," I said.

In the distance some boys were kicking a football around.

Suddenly there was a yell. A group formed and there was more shouting. I could see a boy on the ground holding his head in his hands, another standing over him, his hands on his hips.

"It's Ajoy!" Ranjana yelled.

"He hit Alec!" her friend cried and both of them ran towards the group. Indeed, it was so. It was Alec on the ground. His left eye had around it a rather wonderful purple bruise. He was sobbing. Ajoy was looking around as though daring anyone to say anything, or do anything.

Nobody seemed about to.

Then someone said: "Uh-oh, here comes Mr Slater!"

Ajoy rubbed his hands together in satisfaction. "All right, Mr Alec! That'll teach you to call us names. You stupid idiot!" And he stalked off.

"Wow!" someone said feebly.

"Didn't think he had it in him," someone else said.

"Yeah!" another said, "who would have thought it?"

The teacher came up and asked what was going on. There was an excited babble of voices. Someone pointed to Ajoy. Someone helped Alec to his feet and took him to the infirmary.

Ranjana ran after Ajoy.

"Hey, Ajoy!" she called.

Ajoy stopped. "What?" he growled.

"What was the use of it?" Ranjana said. "You'll only get into trouble now."

"Who cares!" Ajoy said. And he turned and marched off like a little soldier.

Ranjana whispered to herself: "Things like that don't help."

"Maybe so, maybe no," I said. "Sometimes you have to do these things." Not that I approve of violence. But it's like telling little white lies. Sometimes you have to do it, when telling the blunt truth doesn't work. So sometimes when being peaceful and calm doesn't work, you have to use a little fist. I thought Ajoy had done well. Just one *blam!* and with enough force so no one else had interfered and made things worse.

Ranjana was rather quiet the rest of the day. I watched a day in the life of an English school with great interest.

Soon after lunch break we went back to Crescent Drive by bus. Alec was sitting proudly in the front, two boys commenting on the magnificence of his bruise. Ranjana held Ajoy's hand at the back. Ajoy had been called up by the Headmaster after break, and he had a note in his hand he had to show his parents. He was going to be in some trouble.

"You've just got to help Ajoy, Mr Green Devil, sir," Ranjana said to me later in the evening.

Immediately I remembered what Miss Pennyworth had said: "... we have to learn to live together and think of what's good for everyone ..."

"Have you found out if Alec can see you?" Ranjana asked.

"Not yet," I said, "but ..." I was going to say perhaps he can see Tumble or Zielinski, but I stopped myself in time. Miss Pennyworth had said that one special rule we had to obey was that we tell no humans about the rest of us. It was up to the humans to see those of us they could. "But . . ." I said, "I will go and find out right away. Please, not to worry."

She nodded unhappily and went into the house.

I knocked on Zielinski's door.

He opened it after a while muttering, "Who is it? What is it? Don't you know I only work at night?" And when he saw it was me, he said rudely: "Oh you! what you want, you klotz!"

I told him about my meeting with Miss Pennyworth and about how Alec and Ajoy were always fighting.

"Ach! that stupid 'us-them' business humans get into!" Zielinski said.

"What I am asking you, sir, please, is can you help? Is Alec seeing you? If so, you can maybe help him?"

Zielinski shook his head. "No, he don't see me. But I think he sees Tumble. Go talk to Tumble." Then he glowered. "And don't wake me up again so early with some stupid problem."

But although he was so rude, I felt this grumbling gnome had a kind heart underneath.

I couldn't find Tumble anywhere that evening and all next day.

The morning after, I was down amongst the roots of the elm tree looking at the work of the root hairs. I was checking to see if the root cells were all lined up properly and clean. Suddenly the trunk of the tree began to shake and there was a horrible sawing sound.

A saw! Oh no! Was someone cutting down my elm?

I sped up into the trunk. But saw no blades coming through anywhere. There was some huge object rubbing itself against the outside of the trunk, scraping on the bark.

I came out of the tree and saw … an enormous Indian elephant rasping its hide against the trunk, scratching its side. It had the most blissful look on its face.

An elephant?

An Indian elephant in Wimbledon?

Had it escaped from the zoo? By now I knew how strict the rules were in England. You could expect to see an elephant ambling down the road between the cars and buses and rikshaws in Madras, stopping with the traffic at the traffic lights. But you wouldn't expect to see elephants on the streets in London.

But even if it *had* escaped from the zoo, how could it get into the back garden of 32, Crescent Drive? Surely the spaces on the sides of the house were too narrow? It couldn't have come through the house!!

My head began to ache.

Then the elephant chuckled and rolled its eyes wickedly and said: "Man, that feel so-o-o good!"

"Tumble!" I cried.

"The same, the very same," the elephant said and turned into a brownie.

I sat down suddenly feeling very weak. And then began to laugh. I laughed until I cried while Tumble watched, his arms folded across his chest.

When I finally stopped he said: "You okay now, man? So much laughin' kin make you crazy." Then briskly: "Zielinski say you wan' see me."

I wiped my eyes and said: "Yes I was looking for you yesterday. Where are you living?"

But Tumble looked mysterious. "Everywhere, man," he said, "an' no place. But what can I do foh you?"

I told him about Ajoy and Alec. "Zielinski is saying Alec is sometimes seeing you. If so, maybe you can be doing something to make Alec less nasty to Ajoy," I finished.

Tumble snorted. "That Alec!" he said. "I would thrash him good if I could, man. Because he pink he think he something special. Better than brown, yellow an' black."

I thought about how in India, humans who lived in the north and were fair thought they were better than humans who lived in the south, who were dark. But the people who lived in south India thought they were better because they were more educated and had a longer history than the people in the north.

I said: "I have noticed that when people think they are better than others it is because in their hearts they are afraid."

"I suppose that can be true," Tumble said, "but what I could do 'bout that, man?"

I scratched my head. "How is Alec seeing you?" I asked. "I mean is he seeing you like brownie, or elephant or fish or what?"

"Like I am," Tumble said, "like a ball of light."

"And what he is doing when he is seeing you?"

"He try to put me out. He put a bucket of water all over me," Tumble laughed. "But I slip off. And he see me over and over again. He surprise, but he doh ask no question. He jus' accept." He shrugged his shoulders, rolled his brownie eyes and stuck his hands out, palms up and grinned. "He see a ball of light in he back yard he kin do nothin' about."

"Can you talk to him, perhaps?" I said. "Can you ask him what he is being afraid of? Maybe if he is knowing what he is being afraid of, he can stop bullying Ajoy."

Tumble stroked his chin. "I doh think he listen if I speak to him," he said slowly, "but maybe we could try somethin' else. At night in his dream I could take him to the castle of Cobweb an' Dream, and Miss Pennyworth could find out what troublin' he. We done this sometime before with others."

So that night, while I waited on Alec's windowsill, Tumble squeezed into his room like a ray of light through the space on the side of the window and the frame. He slid across the floor and I saw a ball of light dancing on the end of Alec's bed, and heard a faint chuckle.

Then I saw Alec sit up in bed and roll his eyes. I saw him look at the ball of light, and tilt his head to one side as though he was listening. I saw his mouth drop open in surprise, and then he rubbed his eyes again and shook his head.

Then, like a sleep-walker, he got off his bed, put on his dressing-gown, and opened the window. Tumble leaped out, and Alec followed him, carefully climbing down a drainpipe. I followed Alec.

Tumble jumped over the back wall to the Common behind. Alec climbed up after him. I followed. We walked in single file towards the castle of Cobwebs and Dreams. As we walked towards the castle, Alec seemed to become smaller until he was the same size as us. It was most peculiar.

As we walked up the drawbridge, Ching-An rose up out of the moat like a silver wraith in the moonlight. She looked at us as though we were the most boring sight in the world. Then she raised one haughty eyebrow and slipped back into the water without a ripple.

We went through the empty courtyard and the Great Hall to the small room I'd been in ... how long ago *that* seemed. Alec looked around him, his eyes wide and disbelieving. He rubbed his hair till it stood straight up, and shook his head.

"Yoo-hoo, Miss Pennyworth," Tumble called. "Got a fren' to see you."

Alec said: "This is rubbish. Stupid rubbish."

Miss Pennyworth floated in.

Alec nearly jumped out of his skin. Then he began to laugh. "Fairies! What bunk! Yer jus' havin' a dream, Alec me old mate. Nothin' to worry about!"

Miss Pennyworth smiled. "That's right, Alec," she said, "you *are* in a dream. You're in the Castle of Dreams. Do you like it?"

Alec looked around and shrugged. "It's okay, I suppose, for a dream," he said without enthusiasm.

Miss Pennyworth turned and went towards a huge chart on the wall to one side. It was a map of the stars. "Here, come here, Alec," she said.

Alec got up and followed her. He looked at the chart with a little more interest.

"Dreams are very important, Alec," Miss Pennyworth said. "You learn a lot from your dreams, you sort out a lot of problems in dreams, and most of all, dreams are what the real world is made up of."

Alec snorted. "So? That's what you say. What's these stars got to do with dreams, then?"

"Dreams are like the stars," Miss Pennyworth said. "They are always there. When the sun shines in the daytime, you don't see the stars, but they are there anyway, aren't they?"

Alec's eyes widened, and he said, "You mean you can't see your dreams in the daytime, but they're always there?"

"That's just so," Miss Pennyworth said. "Dreams shape your thoughts and your thoughts shape the world."

"What are you going on about?" Alec said.

"Well, how do you suppose buildings are made? Someone thinks up what they want the building to look like, right? Then plans are made, and from the plans buildings are made. But before the thoughts, there were dreams." She turned towards him, walked over to the sofa and sat down.

"How did you get that black eye, Alec?" she said in a friendly way.

Alec touched the bruise around his eye tenderly. "Got it in a fight at school," he said proudly. "I wasn't afraid of the boy Ajoy who gave it to me, neither. I'm going to beat him up good tomorrow." Alec puffed up his chest like a rooster.

"Why did Ajoy hit you?" Miss Pennyworth asked.

"Because I told all me mates at school about the rubbish in the back yard of their house."

I sighed. My wretched sneeze!

"Is there still rubbish in Ajoy's back yard?" Miss Pennyworth said.

"Don't know, didn't look."

"What you saw was an accident," Miss Pennyworth said. "Why did you make up your mind about the Bannerjees after seeing just one accident?"

"It wasn't just one accident," Alec said hotly.

"They're always like that. They act different, they speak different, they eat different and they look different. That's what me Dad says, anyhow."

"So you Dad, he afraid of anythin' different than he!" Tumble said, glowing with a bright anger.

"Me Dad's not afraid of anything!" Alec shouted jumping up. "He's strong and clever. And I've had enough of this stupid dream." He got up and stamped out of the room muttering, "Fairies! Stupid fairies! Yer goin' off your chump, Alec!"

We watched him through the transparent wall of the castle, getting bigger and more human-sized as he walked across the Common.

Tumble muttered under his breath: "He Dad know everythin'. Man!"

Miss Pennyworth sighed and turned to me. "Well, Chellappa. No miracles tonight. It's difficult facing the truth even in your dreams." She sat down. "But it's a start," she said. "We've sown a few seeds in Alec's mind. Let's see if the ideas take root."

Tumble said: "You see how difficult our work is, man?"

I did. I did indeed. Back in India people who were alike lived and worked together and mixed with others only when it was necessary. But here so many different kinds of people who did so many different kinds of work all lived right next door to each other. There was bound to be trouble which would take a while to sort out.

It was a very thoughtful me who slipped into his elm tree that night.

10

Oh, to be in Madras!

THE days flew by, the months flew by. Spring turned to summer, and everywhere flowers bloomed. The elm tree shed brown seeds on the ground. Humans came out of their homes and sat in that gardens in the sunshine, or walked in the park, throwing pebbles into the pond, and not once seeing the Castle of Cobwebs and Dreams.

I began to feel more and more the way I thought an elm tree-devil might feel. And since the elm didn't need as much of my energy to keep healthy as a tamarind tree would, I had a lot of spare time. I spent it with Zielinski, helping him mend broken wings on birds, take care of frogs and insects, and keep the gardens and parks clean.

Ching-An became a little more friendly sometimes, and we talked about India and China. I learned a lot about China from her, and she about India from me. But she never told me how she'd got to London.

Tumble and Miss Pennyworth spent long hours together reading up about shadow people, where they lived now, and what they were doing. Tumble would disappear for many days, looking for them, and come back with reports for Miss Pennyworth. Often they sent for me and I would tell them about all the little folk in India, the apsaras, danavas, daityas, nagins, kinnaras, gandharavs, yakshas, and the hundreds and thousands of others who live in all nooks and crannies of the country taking care of everything from sewing needles to machines, from snails to fish and elephants.

One morning, Ranjana said: "I don't know how you did it, but thank you. Alec's stopped calling Ajoy names. But," she sighed, "Ajoy still doesn't like it here. He still wants to go back to Calcutta."

A few days later I saw Alec hanging on the fence between their houses. Ajoy was digging up a flower bed.

"I see you got a pretty clean garden today," Alec said in a friendly way.

Ajoy just went "Hmmmpf!"

"Say, you don't grow vegetables. Shall I send you

over some of ours, then?" Alec offered.

"Hmmpf," Ajoy said again, got up and slammed his way back into the house.

But I noticed he did look back curiously at Alec before he went.

One day, just as summer began and the sun stayed in the sky for the whole day, warming up the earth, an English girl of about eight, saw me. She was on her swing in the back garden of her house, and I was running an errand for Zielinski. As I hopped over the fence, she shrieked. I stopped. She ran. But her curiosity got the better of her, and soon she was back.

"What's your name?" she asked me when she'd stopped feeling frightened.

"Brum," I said.

"Oh!" she said. "Are you a Brummie?"

And that got *me* confused. It seems that people who come from this city called Birmingham, north of London, are called Brummies. After we had sorted that out, I told her I was from India.

She looked at me carefully and said: "I like your fangs best."

And after that it didn't take long for us to become friends, you can be sure.

One day a Jamaican boy saw Zielinski, and a Punjabi lady saw me and later, an Englishman saw me. He was one of those who give a loud yell and faint dead away over their garden rakes. And then convince themselves they saw nothing at all.

People rarely saw Ching-An or Miss Pennyworth, as they didn't live close to the houses. They hardly ever saw Tumble because he spent a lot of time away, and when he was home, he was changing shape all the time.

Then, one day, on a Sunday morning in May, I was in the back garden of 48, Crescent Drive when I heard voices speaking in Tamil. I hadn't been back in this garden since I'd seen the stone gnomes in the front. It was the home of the Narayans.

"Feels just like Madras today," Mrs Narayan said.

Mr Narayan replied: "Yes, a day like this makes you think of home, doesn't it?"

And quite suddenly, listening to Mr and Mrs Narayan talking in Tamil, about Madras, a great wave of home-sickness washed over me. I felt almost ill and had to sit down on a rock. I found suddenly I was weeping. And here I had been thinking I was beginning to feel like an elm tree-devil!

I went back every day, just to listen to them talking in Tamil. I would sit on their window ledge and sometimes even on top of their T.V. in the evenings.

Everything they said made me think of Madras and every day my longing for home grew greater. I began to dream at night about my tamarind tree in the front garden of Mrs Narayan's father's home in Nungambakkam in Madras.

And the elm tree became restless with my thoughts.

One day I said to Ranjana: "I must go back to Madras."

She shook her head. "You're an elm tree-devil now. There are no elms in Madras."

"I can go back to my tamarind tree," I said stubbornly.

Ranjana, ever practical, said: "And suppose you can't for any reason. What will you do then? You didn't really leave a home behind you to return to. And life here has changed you. You've made a new home here."

I told her I was one thousand, seven hundred and fifty-eight years old and all that time I had lived in or around Madras. How could six months in England have changed me so much?

Ranjana sighed. "You'll see," she said.

As the summer waned, the sun stopped shining for me. The skies always seemed grey. Nothing was interesting, and nothing went right. I quarrelled with Zielinski and snapped at Tumble. I refused to go to the Castle of Cobwebs and Dreams any more. Like Ching-An, I began to sulk.

Summer turned to Autumn and the leaves began to fall. The elm tree told me she wasn't comfortable having me around any more. So many negative thoughts, she said, made her feel weak, and she had to prepare for winter.

I tried to become more cheerful, but there was nothing I could do to stay that way. I took to being in the elm tree only for a little while every day to do the necessary work, and the rest of the time in the woodshed staring at the spades and rakes.

Then, one day, Ranjana said: "We're going to Calcutta for the Christmas holiday. We're going to see if we can get Ajoy into a school in Calcutta."

And I said at once: "I'm coming with you."

"All right," she said. "I'll put you in an airbag and keep you in the aeroplane cabin with us."

After that I began to feel more cheerful. And as the day to leave came nearer, I began to jump and laugh and sing.

Ranjana said: "It's only for a month, so you can come back to London with us."

And I said: "Oh, I won't come back here, I'm sure."

When I told the others, Miss Pennyworth sighed. "So much for our new world," she said. "But you must do what you must do."

Tumble flew into a rage. "Your heart is small and stingy like a little pebble," he roared. "You just go an' doh come back, you hear?"

Ching-An sighed. "I wish I could come with you."

"Why not?" I said. "You can get to China quicker from Calcutta than from London. You could be a day and a night out of water with no trouble."

"Ah, but I don't want to have to spend any time in some strange Indian river waiting to find out a way to get back to China," she said. "I want to go straight back."

Zielinski grunted and said: "You'll be back."

My elm tree wept, but what could I do? I had to do what I had to do.

And I wept too, when I said goodbye to my friends.

I will not tell you about getting to the airport, or flying in that unnatural way, except to say, inside the passenger cabin it's much warmer than it is in the baggage hold, and your ears don't hurt so much. Also, that one air-hostess saw me and spilled a whole tray of drinks over some large, noisy passengers, and for a while there was a lot of confusion ... and I suppose I really must confess that after nearly eleven months I sneezed again ... it had to do with those fizzy drinks they serve you ... I'll leave it to your imagination to tell you what happened next – I cannot speak of my shame again. I thank Lord Vishnu the Preserver that we didn't crash.

But I will tell you how I felt when we stepped out of the aeroplane at Dum Dum Airport outside Calcutta.

I thought I would simply die of joy.

It wasn't Madras, but it was India. Oh, the sights, the sounds, the smells! They were all of home. The people of Calcutta looked different to the people of

Madras. They talked differently, and dressed differently. But there is something that is India about Calcutta, as there is something that is India about Madras, or Delhi, or Shillong, or about the Punjab, or Gujarat or Himachal. And that something meant home, home, *home*.

It was dirty, it was hot, it was uncomfortable. But it was home. My frozen elm-tree blood began to warm up, and I leapt high in the air, shouting: *"Abbabbaba! Abbabbaba!"*

Yes, I did fall down nearly dead with the effort. But it was on Indian earth.

Ajoy and Ranjana's grandparents lived in a flat in a crowded street in Ballygunge. But for all the crowds and the noise and the bustle, it was easier to get around Calcutta than it was in London. Ranjana found out the timings of trains to Madras, and asked if she could go shopping with her grandfather's cook, one day. She got the cook to get us down to Howrah station, and he put me on the right train.

I was saddest of all to leave Ranjana. She was such a very good friend and I thought this was goodbye. I would never see her again. But already I was thinking ahead to Madras.

Madras, Madras, Madras.

My home. Oh, wonderful tamarind tree, we would finish our Battle of Surrender . . . Oh, my school in the Adyar Banyan, oh, Guru Ramachandran, oh, my father and my mother, my friends, Rajappa and Muthaiyya, oh, my brothers and sisters, I was coming home!

Wouldn't they all be surprised to see me! What stories I would have to tell them! I could imagine the look of wonder on their faces as I told them about Miss Pennyworth, and about Zielinski and Ching-An. What would they make of Tumble?

I looked out of the window and the train clacked and rushed southwards. But I saw nothing. My heart and my mind were already in Madras.

We came into Madras Central station early in the morning the next day.

And I fell out of the train, and kissed the earth.

I hardly heard the voices around me. I hardly saw the people. I was in too much of a hurry. Nungambakkam, oh Nungambakkam. My tamarind tree, I'm coming home.

I sat on a cycle rikshaw going my way, but it was too slow. So I hopped off and got on a bus. But even that was too slow. So I got off and began to run.

Up Nungambakkam High Road, through Haddows Road, down College Road, turn right ... and I was on Anderson Road, Nungambakkam. And then running, panting, out of breath, I was in front of 84B, Anderson Road!

And there was my tamarind tree, nodding green,

and rough in the morning sun. My heart burst with pride as I looked at it.

I ran up to it, like a father to a lost child. "I've come back for you," I cried, "I've found you again. Let's finish our Great Battle, my tamarind."

But, then, oh, Shiva! I heard a voice, a great booming voice cry out from the tree: "Who would break the Law of Brahma? Can there be more than one devil living in a tree?"

I fell back, stunned. How could I have been so stupid? How could I have been so blind? Of course, another devil would have moved into my tree! Guru Ramachandran used to say: "Water has no time to practise falling!" Miss Pennyworth often said: "Time and tide wait for no man."

Weakly, I said: "Come out, Oh revered brahmarakshasa, so I may embrace my brother."

And who was it that fell out of my tree, but my old friend Rajappa! He looked well and happy, and as handsome as before.

Oh, how we embraced each other, how we wept.

"Brother Chellappa! Aiyo! Where have you been?" Rajappa said. "But how ill you look! What has happened to you?"

"Ill?" I said.

"Yes, ill. Unwell." He held me at arm's length. "Where has all your colour gone? You look like a dried leaf!"

"Why?" I said, surprised, "am I not green?"

"Come, look at yourself, dear friend," Rajappa said. "Come into the house and we'll look in a mirror."

So we went into the house, and stood side by side in front of a mirror in the bedroom.

It was true! I was no longer the deep rich green I used to be. I was a pale green, almost yellow. And I was even taller and thinner than I used to be. Even my eyes looked washed out. No longer were they that handsome ruby red . . . they were pink! How was it I had not noticed before?

I turned to Rajappa, aghast. Beside me he looked so healthy and so dark and so rich.

"You are a shadow of your former self, dear friend," Rajappa said. "You even talk strangely. Come, tell me how this came to be."

So we sat under the tamarind tree and I told him all that happened. He listened, with his eyes getting wider and wider. He shook his head often, and clucked disapprovingly several times. When I told him how I had become an elm tree-devil, and how easy it had been, he began to move away from me.

I tried to tell him about Miss Pennyworth's dream for all people to live together in harmony. But I couldn't. Rajappa would never understand what all those far away things had to do with him and, anyway, people lived together pretty well over here.

And besides, if I wanted to go back to being a tamarind tree-devil, what had those ideas to do with me?

Finally I said: "So, here I am, Rajappa, and you are in my tree. Perhaps I should try to find another tamarind tree."

And to my utter astonishment, he spat on the ground.

"Chhi, chhi, chhi! Thoo! You have broken your caste. You are no longer a pulliyamachedi brahmarakshasa. How can you occupy a tamarind tree? And what is this elm tree? Are you an elm-devil? Or are you a little bit of an elm-devil and a little bit of a tamarind-devil? You have no caste any more."

Caste?

Why! I hadn't thought of caste for almost a year now!

For a moment I felt like laughing. The whole idea of caste was so strange, and that anyone should take it seriously was very funny. I put my arm around his shoulder and said: "Rajappa!"

But he pulled away from me.

"Don't touch me until you are purified," he said.

Purified?

I stared at him.

How absurd it was that a special bath and priests chanting prayers over me, would make me pure! I didn't feel impure or dirty or wrong for anything I'd done.

And suddenly all my happiness at having come home was gone like a bit of dry breeze. Rajappa's way of thinking was not mine any more. Something in me had changed and would never come back. And it wasn't just my tamarind tree cells, my tamarind tree blood. It was more than that. It was as though my eyes saw further left and light, up and down, than they had ever seen before, and I would never be able to blinker my eyes again.

Then I realized I was feeling very, very angry. How dare Rajappa judge me! Who was he to tell me that I had done *wrong*! I wanted to leap up and shout: "Why you stupid, narrow-minded brahmarakshasa. Who are you to sit in judgement over me! It's *you* who are wrong to think of stupid, narrow-minded things like caste and bathing and purification . . ." I opened my mouth . . . and shut it again.

There I was getting stuck in thinking someone had to be wrong if I was to be right. *That* was stupid. And I suddenly felt very, very tired. How difficult it was to stop thinking about 'right-wrong', 'win-lose', 'us-them', 'enemy-friend'. Wearily, I said: "Rajappa, I see we're on different roads now. I cannot agree that I am impure because of what I have done. And I cannot explain to you why I don't feel I've done wrong. I hope some day you'll go to foreign lands, meet people who think the very opposite of the way you do, and find out that they are not wrong to think so. Then, perhaps you won't think of caste and purification."

Rajappa frowned. He couldn't understand why something so natural and normal as caste and purification should be questioned. A year ago I would have felt the same way as Rajappa! "I don't understand you, my friend," he said sadly. "You are not the devil I knew. How can you live with foreign barbarians and take on foreign ways of thinking, and still consider yourself a brahmarakshasa?"

"My dear Rajappa," I said, tears in my eyes, "you are not wrong to think the way you do, because that's the way you must think to live here, and you don't know any different. But, then, I am not wrong either to see things a little differently. I am still a brahmarakshasa, perhaps now of a different kind. The reason I can think so, is because I've seen that people in far away lands, though different from us in many ways, are all, also Brahma's children, just like us."

And I said goodbye and turned away, leaving him staring at my back. As I left I put my hand on the tamarind tree. There was, for a while, nothing. I could feel nothing. Then, faintly, far away, I heard the familiar tamarind tree root-beat. I smiled. I could be a tamarind tree-devil again, if I wanted to.

But, just then, I didn't want to. I had much to think about. I had to get away from the house, from the tamarind tree, from my memories of home.

11

Wandering and Wondering

F OR many days I wandered around in Madras, breathing in the sights and smells of the Burma Market, listening to the sounds of people talking Tamil, looking at all the familiar places, St Thomas Mount, the Viceregal Lodge, the Red Hills around the city. I stood outside the School of Music and listened to the sounds of the veena and the violin. And I wondered why I wasn't looking for a tamarind tree to live in.

Then, I went out to Chennapatnam where my first tamarind tree had battled me so many hundreds of years ago. It had died and other trees stood in its place.

I went to all the other villages, and all the places in the city in which I had ever lived and worked. Everything looked the same, yet everything was so different. Could one year in a foreign land have changed the world so much?

Then, one day I took a bus to the Theosophical Society, and stood below a hedge looking at the Adyar Banyan. I thought of the many classrooms in its many aerial roots, and of the many young brahmarakshasas sneezing at plants and brooms and brushes. I imagined them studying the rates of rising sap, the insects and pesticides which destroyed the trees and all those other important things brahmarakshasas must know. I wondered if they knew of the Dutch elm beetle which was such a curse to elm trees.

I watched brahmarakshasas scurrying around on the lawns on their way home, avoiding humans. And I saw humans strolling about not seeing the little devils darting between their legs. I suddenly thought that we shadow folk know so much about humans and humans know so little about us.

And I remembered Ranjana saying once: "Ajoy says the trouble with being an Indian in England, is that we know so much about English people, and they know so little about us."

You will wonder, Guru Ramachandran, if you

should read this account, that I didn't come to touch your feet. I saw you in the distance, but my heart was too heavy with Rajappa's words to speak any more to anyone about anything.

And I turned away.

Then one day in Mylapore I saw a young tamarind tree, just ready to receive a tree-devil. It swayed sweetly in the sun, and seemed to call to me. I went up to it and put my hand on its bark. I felt the root pulse beat, and waited to feel the excitement in me which always came at the thought of a new tamarind tree. But nothing happened. And I couldn't make up my mind about whether I wanted to make my home in this tree or not.

For several days I waited around the tree, hoping I could feel sure about what I should do.

Then, one night as I lay under the stars looking at the moon, I heard Miss Pennyworth's voice, floating between the clouds, say: "People have always longed for a new world, new ways of thinking, new ways of behaving." And I heard Tumble's chuckles in my ears. "We all will have be bigger in we heart than we use to be," he said. Then he shouted: "You heart is small and stingy like a pebble!" I saw Ching-An's sullen face, and heard Zielinski's grumble as he stomped around tending to sparrows and frogs.

And through a mist of cobwebs and dreams I heard my elm tree call.

My elm tree!

Then I knew I could not leave a tree I lived in. By the code of brahmarakshasas I was tied to it through its life. And, as I lay looking at the clouds in the Indian night sky, I knew in my heart I was a brahmarakshasa, and would always be. But a brahmarakshasa who would have to stretch himself more than brahmarakshasas usually do. It had nothing to do with caste, except perhaps that caste was a way to make sure you did not have to stretch to hold something new. Caste was a way of being clean and healthy, of preserving the environment, of knowing who you were and your place in life. But is was also a way of being safe.

I remembered Miss Pennyworth saying: "The test of living is how big you can be, how much of life you can hold."

And I knew then, that I would go back to London.

12

Going Home

THE next day I went to visit my mother and father. They were old and almost deaf and blind, and lived in The Homes for Respected Ones which were in the palm trees on Injanbakkam beach. After five thousand years of service to trees, they rested five years in the Homes before Brahma called them back to his heaven, gave them new lives, and new jobs and sent them back to Earth.

They were happy I had come, and we talked about my brothers and sisters who all had their own tamarind trees. Sister Vijaylaxmi had got married while I was away and they had tried very hard to find me.

Sister Anandlaxmi had had her second baby whom they were naming Chellappa after me. Brother Ranganathan had had his twelfth Great Battle of Surrender ... My parents asked how I'd been and how my work was going. I said it was going well.

"Where is your new tree, my son?" my father asked.

I hesitated, then I said: "In a place called London, Father."

"And where is that, my son?"

"Some miles to the north of Madras," I said, "and some miles west." I could not tell them more. And sometimes, if you are wise, a little lie works better than the truth, for if I told them my story, would they understand any better than had Rajappa?

"It is well, my son," my mother said, peering at me. "But you look a little tired. You should take time off for family festivities and rest from your work sometimes. When will you come to see us again?"

And I said: "Next year, Mother, at the same time." And I knew I would. I would come back every year so my heart did not shrink to just the world in London.

My mother said: "Brahma's will shall always be done."

And as I left them, I thought: "If it is Brahma's will, that I live in London, and work with Miss Pennyworth getting people to live together, then he surely wants to create the kind of world my parents couldn't have dreamed about."

I visited my brothers and sisters and their families in their tamarind trees, and some part of me envied them their safety. Would I ever be like them again? I thought not.

And one day I took a train to Calcutta.

Ranjana was delighted to see me back. She understood at once how I felt.

"At first Mum and Dad were so happy to be in Calcutta, but now Dad's just itching to get on the plane and get back to work in London," she said.

She asked me about Madras, and I told her about Rajappa and caste, and about my elm tree calling. I told her about our family. But, of course I couldn't tell her about Miss Pennyworth and Zielinski and Tumble and Ching-An.

I asked about Ajoy.

"Ajoy's coming back to London with us," she said. "Our cousins think us pretty strange too. We talk different, we think different, we dress different. About the only thing that's the same is the food we eat and, then, too, we eat many more different kinds of food than they do. Ajoy doesn't fit here any more than he does in England. But he thinks if he stays here now he'll become somehow *smaller*."

I nodded; I understood that feeling. I said, "There will be a time when we know that under our differences we are all the same. Then our hearts will become bigger and we'll have a whole new world."

We were back in London in under a month after we'd left, which was just as well for me, because I was beginning to feel weak again.

It was strange coming back to this cold, damp grey country ... because it suddenly felt like home. And that really confused me.

When he saw me, Tumble turned into a grasshopper and leapt up to the chimneys. "Man, you come back, you come back!" he shouted, and producing a violin began playing an English tune using two legs, and with four legs did a Trinidad shuffle.

Miss Pennyworth said, "Ah!" in a pleased way, and hurried off, but not before I'd seen there were tears in her eyes.

Ching-An said bluntly: "Why did you come back?"

"Because," I said, "I didn't want my heart to shrink."

She looked thoughtful as she slipped back into the water.

My elm tree shivered with happiness.

Zielinski said grumpily: "I told you so, you klotz!"

And, Guru Ramachandran, I will tell you this, I was glad to have been told.

For while it's not easy being a devil, Brum-um-um, oh, my friends and brothers and sisters in Madras, I yum-um-um.

THE BEST-KEPT SECRET
Emily Rodda

The arrival of the fairground carousel, surrounded by its neat red and white painted fence, with a tent guarding its entrance, was a complete mystery to the residents of Marley Street. Where had it come from? How had it appeared so quickly? And why was the music so haunting, beckoning all to come and look? Jo is determined to have a ride, even though she senses the ride may take her into danger, into an unknown world . . . the world of the future.

THE TOBY MAN
Dick King-Smith

Young Tod Golightly knows what a highwayman *should* say and do, but finds it's more difficult than it sounds. Being so young and inexperienced, people don't take him seriously. Then he gathers about himself a team of unlikely accomplices – a wise old donkey, a large dog, a magpie and a cunning ferret. Together they pull off a daring robbery, which turns Tod into the terror of the Great West Road. But the Bow Street Runners are after this dangerous criminal and determined to make him pay – with his life. How will his animals friends be able to help him now?

BIG IGGY
Kaye Umansky

When Large Lizzy decides it's time she had a bit of peace and quiet, Big Iggy – the smallest dragon – and his brother all take off into the big wide world. But Big Iggy's first flight ends with a crash landing into a tree – and a huge adventure.

RT, MARGARET AND THE RATS OF NIMH
Jane Leslie Conly

When Margaret and her brother RT get lost in the forests surrounding Thorn Valley, help comes from an unexpected quarter when the super-rats of NIMH come to their rescue. Margaret and RT must return home before winter sets in, but the incredible events of their summer in the valley become the biggest secret they have ever had to keep.

The third thrilling story in this classic trilogy about the rats of NIMH.

WOLF
Gillian Cross

Cassy finds her mother living in a squat with her boyfriend Lyall and his son Robert. Lyall has devised a theatrical event for children on wolves, and Cassy is soon deeply involved in presenting it. Perhaps too involved – for she begins to sense a very real and terrifying wolf stalking her.

TWIN AND SUPER TWIN
Gillian Cross

Ben, David and Mitch had only meant to start the Wellington Street Gang's bonfire, not blow up all their fireworks as well. But what is worse is what happens to David's arm in the process. Until, that is, they realize that this extraordinary event could be very useful in their battles with the Wellington Street Gang.

A RAT'S TALE
Tor Seidler

Montague Mad-Rat lives in a sewer in New York City, where his family are impoverished but creative. His life is very sheltered until he meets Isabel Moberly Rat who changes all this. Isabel is a wharf rat, enjoying a much richer lifestyle, but Montague realizes that her home will soon be turned into a car park and, because of his love for her, plans to act immediately. But he is hindered by his background, so how can he possibly save Isabel and Ratdom, and win her love at the same time?

THE GOLDEN JOURNEY
John Rowe Townsend

Eleni has always been different from all the other people on her island but she never dreamt that she would be chosen by the gods to be the messenger to save her island from a war that is destroying them.

DODOS ARE FOREVER
Dick King-Smith

Once upon a time (about 300 years ago) Dodos lived happily on an island in the Indian Ocean. Then one day Man arrived (and more importantly, rats arrived too) and the happy, peaceful life of the Dodos would never be the same again. This is the riveting, funny, tragic tale of the demise of the Dodos – and of one small group of birds that (according to Dick King-Smith) made their escape and set up a new colony on a nearby island.

THE FOX OF SKELLAND

Rachel Dixon

Samantha's never liked the old custom of Foxing Day – the fox costume especially gives her the creeps. So when Jason and Rib, children of the new publicans at The Fox and Lady, find the costume and Jason wears it to the fancy-dress disco, she's sure something awful will happen.

Then Sam's old friend Joseph sees the ghost of the Lady and her fox. Has she really come back to exact vengeance on the village? Or has her appearance got something to do with the spate of burglaries in the area?

THE SHADOW-CAGE AND OTHER TALES OF THE SUPERNATURAL

Philippa Pearce

Quite ordinary things turn out to be haunted in the world Philippa Pearce creates – a funny little statue, an old biscuit barrel, a nursery cupboard – and in quite ordinary circumstances. Memories of past unhappiness can cling to a place connected with them. A man out for his evening exercise can find his hatred of his brother suddenly taking shape as a running companion. And human passions can even reach beyond the grave if they're powerful enough – a mother's longing for her daughter's return, an old man desperate at the neglect of his once-cherished garden. These ten stories are written with all the fine perception for which their author is celebrated.

THE SHADOW-GUESTS

Joan Aiken

The deep mystery surrounding the disappearance of Cosmo's mother and elder brother had never been solved. Then peculiar things began to happen to Cosmo at the old mill house where he was staying. Strangers appeared and only Cosmo could see them. What did they want? Where, or *when*, did they come from?

ESIO TROT
Roald Dahl

Mr Hoppy is in love with Mrs Silver. But Mrs Silver has eyes
only for Alfie, her pet tortoise. How can he ever compete with
such a rival? He comes up with a bold plan to win his lady's
love, involving some clever riddles and a whole army of tor-
toises. Will Mr Hoppy's patience be rewarded? And what's to
become of Alfie?

A highly comic and unusual love story.

JUST FERRET
Gene Kemp

Owen Hardacre, otherwise known as Ferret, has been
dragged around the country by his artist father and been to so
many schools that he doesn't expect much from Cricklepit
Combined School. But when he makes friends with Beany and
Minty and gains the respect of Sir, things begin looking
up . . . even the reading!

Meet Ferret, his friends *and* enemies in this fifth story of the
pupils of Cricklepit Combined School.

DID YOU THINK I WOULD LEAVE
YOU CRYING?
Moira Miller

This collection of sensitive and moving stories traces the effects
of conflict and compassion across the years; the friendship, the
heroism and the cruelty of war.

ANASTASIA MORNINGSTAR

Hazel Hutchins

If Sarah and Ben hadn't been in the grocery store that day, they wouldn't have seen Derek Henshaw trying to steal a water pistol. And they wouldn't have seen him being turned into a frog by the woman who worked there. Anastasia Morningstar looked quite ordinary (and she certainly had a very ordinary job) but Sarah and Ben soon learned that she could do some very *extraordinary* things . . .

THE WEATHER WITCH

Paul Stewart

Clee Manor is hardly the kind of place that young Londoners Kerry and Joe want to spend the summer. But as direct descendants of the sixteenth-century witch who was responsible for the disappearance of the village of Cleedale, they find themselves drawn into the house's mysterious past.

It is only when they discover the long-lost village and encounter the Weather Witch herself, however, that they begin to understand the danger and awesome power they face.

ACE

Dick King-Smith

Singled out from birth by an unusual marking on his side, Ace is a very special pig. He seems to understand everything Farmer Tubbs says, and soon becomes one of the most popular members of the farmyard. With the help of the other animals, Ace gradually begins to make himself at home in the farmhouse itself where Megan, the queenly Corgi, reigns supreme. She is *not* amused. A pig who watches television? Whatever next!

But Ace is not a descendant of the Sheep-Pig for nothing, and there are yet stranger things to come.

GHOSTS THAT HAUNT YOU

ed. Adian Chambers

A nightmarish monster that lurks in dark places; demonic boys with blood on their minds; a sad old monk lost between worlds; bumps, squeaks and terror in the moonlight. Sometimes horrifying, sometimes funny, these ten ghost stories all involve young people in some way and will keep readers enthralled for hours.

CHARLOTTE SOMETIMES

Penelope Farmer

When Charlotte goes off to boarding school, she suffers from all the confusion and shyness of a new girl. At first she thinks this is why she has difficulty in remembering names and faces. But then she realizes that something very odd has happened: somehow she's slipped back to 1918 and become a girl called Clare. Being Charlotte only sometimes causes terrible problems, but what is she to do about it?